Amelia.

Her eyes were alive with happiness, her smiling bottom lip caught just slightly under her top teeth. Of its own volition, Ross's heart started pounding and his breathing quickened, deepened. He didn't want her to move away from him, but to move into his aching arms.

"My mother called that sky-blue-pink. Incredible," she said of the colorful sky.

Ross couldn't seem to get his eyes to look at anything but her. "Yeah, incredible," he agreed, staring at Amelia's peaches-and-cream skin. He'd touched that skin the night of the fire, swearing as he did that it meant goodbye. He'd thought it was. But she was every temptation he'd ever faced all rolled into one lovely package.

"We'd better get going," he said, in danger of dragging her into his arms and kissing her. He jumped off the tailgate, but as he turned back to urge her to get a move on, she slid to the ground in front of him. The most natural and stupid thing he could have done was to lean down and cover her upturned mouth with his. And he did.

Books by Kate Welsh

Love Inspired

For the Sake of Her Child #39
Never Lie to an Angel #69
A Family for Christmas #83
Small-Town Dreams #100
Their Forever Love #120
*The Girl Next Door #156
*Silver Lining #173

*Laurel Glen

KATE WELSH,

a two-time winner of Romance Writers of America's coveted Golden Heart Award and a finalist for RWA's RITA® Award in 1999, lives in Havertown, Pennsylvania, with her husband of thirty years. When not at work in her home-office creating stories and the characters that populate them, Kate fills her time with other creative outlets. There are few crafts she hasn't tried at least once or a sewing project that hasn't been a delicious temptation. Those ideas she can't resist grace her home or those of friends and family.

As a child she was often the "scriptwriter" in neighborhood games of make-believe. Kate turned back to storytelling when her husband challenged her to write down the stories that were in her head. With Jesus so much a part of her life, Kate found it natural to incorporate Him in her writing. Her goal is to entertain her readers with wholesome stories of the love between two people the Lord has brought together and to teach His truths while she entertains.

Silver Lining

Kate Welsh

Love Inspired®

Published by Steeple Hill Books™

STEEPLE HILL BOOKS

**Steeple
Hill**

ISBN 0-373-87180-5

SILVER LINING

Copyright © 2002 by Kate Welsh

Visit us at www.steeplehill.com

Printed in U.S.A.

Come to me all you who are heavy laden
and I will give you rest.
—*Matthew* 11:28

To the other two Northern Loons—
the best people I ever ran away with.

Prologue

❧

The watcher stood unobserved at the edge of the crowd. Ross Taggert held the horses steady as his beloved daughter, Hope, climbed into the old carriage. Ross's new son-in-law, Jeff Carrington, helped her a bit from behind, then carefully climbed to sit by his bride's side. Marley's girl had cleaned up real pretty for her wedding day. Hope wore a soft-looking white gown and the veil Marley had worn the day she'd been foolish enough to marry Ross Taggert.

Hope beamed a smile at her new husband while he settled next to her and looped an arm around her back. That Carrington boy had certainly surprised the daylights out of a church full of people by walking up the aisle to meet Hope. It had been quite a guilt reliever to see him out of that wheelchair.

Jeff hadn't been the target of the damaged girth

any more than Hope had been the intended victim of those badly stacked hay bales that fell on her. A crying shame, but it couldn't be helped. They'd gotten in the way. The vandalism had been aimed at the ones responsible for Marley's death—Ross and his son, Cole.

Up till now, it had been enough, almost satisfying, that Ross had lost his son over Marley's death and that Cole had lost his family and Laurel Glen. But then Cole came home trying to make peace with his father. They deserved nothing good in their lives, and that's how it was going to be.

The watcher slid deeper into the laughing, confetti-throwing crowd. There was no use in brooding today. Today was a day of celebration. The new plan was better. The watcher smiled, too, just like the rest of the crowd, but for a more personal reason. Little did Ross and Cole Taggert know that retribution was at hand. They'd still pay.

This new plan would be slower and draw to a more satisfying conclusion than the original idea of killing Ross outright would have. Both men would lose what they treasured most. Ross—his farm and his son for all time. Cole—his hard-earned reputation and his freedom. They'd be alive to suffer endlessly and Marley, beloved Marley, would be avenged at last.

Chapter One

~⟨≈~

Ross hotfooted it downstairs. He was late starting his day, but that was one advantage he'd always liked about being his own boss. There was no one to take him to task. Of course at eighteen when he'd had to take over Laurel Glen's reins, he'd felt only the burden of stepping into his father's shoes—shoes he'd feared he could never fill.

At the landing, he stopped to gaze out the window that overlooked Laurel Glen. Where had the years gone? It seemed like just yesterday that he'd been the young eager groom bringing his own beautiful wife home to Laurel House. But Marley was long dead, and yesterday he'd given their daughter in marriage. So much time had passed in what felt like the blink of an eye.

Shaking his head, Ross turned from the view and started off for breakfast still thinking of his life. He didn't feel old enough to have a married twenty-seven-year-old daughter. Or a son nearly thirty. *He* felt thirty even though he'd been nineteen when Cole was born. In any math class, this left him knocking on the door of the half-century mark. Maybe feeling so young was the reason he couldn't seem to get a handle on being a father to Cole.

Or maybe it's been so many years since you acted like a father that Cole doesn't want one anymore.

Ross silenced the voice in his head. He refused to consider that it was too late for them. He stopped in the foyer at the gilt-edged mirror hanging there and studied himself for a long moment, but his thoughts drifted and mixed with his other problems. If having a few white hairs would give Cole a true father figure, all he had to do was hang around a little while longer. Because if things kept on the way they were at Laurel Glen, Ross would have snowy-white hair by year's end.

Minutes later he entered the sunny breakfast room where the family ate most meals. "Morning, beautiful," he said to his sister Meg as he bent to kiss her smooth cheek. She sat at the table, as usual picking at her breakfast and nursing a cup of coffee, probably her third. Meg wasn't a morning person, but since returning to Laurel Glen to help him raise the kids, she insisted on being at the breakfast table before anyone.

Meg looked up and smiled. "I wondered if you were going to sleep all day," she admonished, her eyes sparkling with youth and good cheer. "Cole's long gone. He went to look at that practice he's thinking of buying."

"Good. It's a smart move," Ross said as he sat down and smiled his thanks at Ruth Ann, Laurel House's cook. Then, without further ado, he dug into the pancakes and scrapple Ruth Ann had put in front of him.

"Don't let silence from Cole fool you. He was glad for your advice even if he hasn't said so." His sister cleared her throat. "I wanted to talk to you about an idea that's been proposed to me," she said.

Ross looked up. "Proposed?" he asked hopefully.

"Now don't get that look. It's nothing to do with a man. While I was on my cruise, I met a photographer. Well, *she* is actually a photojournalist. We hit it off quite well and we've kept in touch. After a lot of talk about Chester County and its rich history, she wanted to see it. So she proposed an idea for a book to her publisher. It's on the lives of the founding fathers of the county and what their descendants are doing today. They're very interested. I've asked the historical society if she can do her research there, and they've agreed. So she's on her way and she's going to stay here."

"No."

Meg blinked. "What do you mean, no? I already said she's on her way. I wasn't asking permission for a friend to stay here. I didn't know it was necessary."

His sister didn't just look annoyed—she *was* annoyed. And Ross couldn't blame her. Meg had given up a promising Broadway career to raise his children. He'd never understood why she'd done it but when he'd contacted her about Marley's death, Meg was on the next train home and she'd never considered leaving. By the time Hope reached adulthood, Meg's chance to succeed on Broadway was pretty much over. And here he was denying her the freedom to have a friend visit.

"I'm sorry," he said immediately. "Of course your friend is welcome," Ross said then thought of all that could go wrong. Thought of all the accidents and mistakes that had plagued Laurel Glen in the last months. Thought about the rumors that were chipping away at his reputation and his client base. "This just isn't a good time to have a reporter hanging around. That's all."

Meg raised an imperious brow. It was a family trait and irritating as—

"Did I say reporter? Sometimes you hear what you want to hear. I *said* she's a photojournalist. She does coffee table books and high-priced calendar work. She's been commissioned to do travelogues for several high-end travel agencies and a couple of island nations trying to boost their tourist trade. And she's a very nice Christian woman who would never print anything that would hurt Laurel Glen, or anyone else for that matter."

"Oh, she's a Christian. That makes everything so

much better," he said sarcastically. "Ever consider how many people have been persecuted over the years in the name of God?"

"She isn't coming here to persecute anyone. She's coming to take pictures of places that have stood the test of time and to write a book on how the families that own them have endured the years. I want you to make time to talk with her and show her around the operation since our family will be one of those featured in the book."

"No. Please just keep her out of my hair. I have too much to do right now."

"Ross, you're running yourself ragged. Why are you having such a hard time replacing Hope? Are you sure you're not being too particular?"

"Hope is one of the best trainers in the business, and it's tough to replace the best. I've interviewed several men but none of their methods or reputations were up to Laurel Glen standards. Hope's agreed to take over the hiring when she gets back and she has a line on someone Jeff met on the circuit. A Charlie Larson. I vaguely remember hearing the name but I can't place where or when. Anyway, Jeff was impressed, and that's good enough for me. She's trying to find this wonder, talk to him and get him down here if she thinks we should hire him. But until then, I'm stuck with two jobs unless Hope can fill in." He smiled, thinking of how happy his little girl had been when he'd seen her last. "But she's a little busy right now."

Meg, too, smiled. "Where did Jeff take her on their honeymoon, by the way? Has Cole said?"

Ross grimaced. "The day Cole confides in me before he talks something over with you, I'll fly flags from every window of Laurel House."

Meg patted his hand. "He's coming around. Just keep showing him that you respect the changes he's made in his life and sooner or later he'll reciprocate. He wouldn't be here if he didn't want a relationship with you."

"Maybe he's just come home to punish me for Marley's death. Ever think of that?" Ross sighed, his appetite gone. "Listen, I'm running too late. I'd better get going or I'll be up till the cows come home."

Meg chuckled. "We don't have cows. And don't think the subject of Amelia Howard's book is over. I want your cooperation."

Ross walked into the tack room and slammed the door. Was he going to have to fire every single person working at Laurel Glen just to weed out the idiot? He scrubbed his face with his hand, trying to calm down. But it was tough. Of all the idiotic stupid mistakes to make around animals, leaving a pan of antifreeze laying around was about the dumbest. The horses would have gotten to it if they'd been turned out into that paddock as they usually were. This was just plain unforgivable!

Some would say he was lucky it had only been a

couple of cats and three kittens that were poisoned, and he knew he was. But those little creatures had hurt no one and kept the vermin population down to a manageable number. They were members of the team and they'd deserved better. He paced the length of the small room, trying to calm down. But he'd just spent the last two hours with Cole trying to make their last minutes less frightening and painful, and it was hard to put it out of his mind. Just as burying those little furry bodies was going to stick with him for some time to come.

"Dad?" he heard Cole yell.

"In here!"

Cole pushed the door open and stuck his head in. "Try to calm down. Your blood pressure must be through the roof. I'm going up to the house to get cleaned up. Sorry I couldn't do more than put them out of their misery."

"No need to apologize. If you hadn't realized what the symptoms meant so quickly, I wouldn't have gone looking for the antifreeze and we could have lost horses and not just a few barn cats and kittens."

"I guess," Cole said but didn't sound convinced.

"It stinks either way," Ross admitted.

Cole sighed. "It sure does, and so far none of those boneheads will own up to leaving it out in the open that way. Donovan can't remember telling anyone specifically to dispose of it, either. He just made it a general order for someone to do it."

"And isn't that getting to be a familiar refrain. It's just hard to believe anyone could be that stupid."

"True. Listen, Harv Peterson was complaining to Doc Brennan that he has some feral cats out back of his place. I'll see what I can do about moving the kittens over here."

Ross nodded. "Good. Meanwhile, I'm going to get this place in order. It's a mess. I've been telling Donovan to get someone to straighten up in here for weeks. Like my daddy used to say, 'If a job's worth doing, do it right and do it yourself!'"

"Sounds more like Granny Taggert," Cole muttered and left.

"It was," Ross whispered to the empty room. When Granny died, Cole had been in the military school and hadn't been allowed to come home for the funeral. It was another sore point between them. Another piece of proof that he'd been a lousy father.

When the judge had turned down Ross's request for Cole to be allowed to attend Granny's funeral, Ross had decided it would be better for Cole to learn about her death and burial after the fact. Ross had been afraid Cole would try to do something foolish like go AWOL and attend anyway, and he hadn't wanted to tempt his son to get himself in even more trouble. That had been a huge mistake.

Ross shook his head and turned his attention to the tack room, needing a mindless task and something he could fix. He set himself to untangling reins and lunging lines that had been tossed here and there. He hung them neatly where they belonged. Finally he got to a box of spare tack parts. He'd been meaning to find a better way to organize the parts so he'd know what he had and what he needed to order. After nailing several ten-penny nails in a board and mounting it, he started cutting away the pieces of leather and webbing still attached to the various rings, buckles and such.

He worked steadily, cleaning each piece then hanging it on a nail, sorting for size and use as he went along. Then he picked up a badly rotted girth with pristine buckles. At first Ross thought he had to be wrong. This couldn't be the one he'd tossed in the box in February after repairing his saddle following Jeff's accident.

The leather on the discarded piece was far more disintegrated than it had been then. He was sure of it. Ross examined it carefully. This *was* the same girth. He remembered how odd it had seemed that the buckles had been barely used. He was sure no other girth had broken in this way before or since.

He stared at it, then examined the articles around it. The ones underneath were rotted or oddly discolored, as was the place where the girth had looped partially over the torn end. He gave it a good yank, and it tore halfway across.

How could this be? With a feeling of grave foreboding, he brought the girth to his nose and inhaled.

Even after six months the chemical smell was unmistakable.

Stunned, Ross sank on a stool and stared at the evidence that only now explained so much. Six months ago, Hope, who was never careless around the horses, had apparently saddled a horse with a badly worn girth. Jeff Carrington had ridden the horse and been thrown, resulting in paralysis for six long months. Ross had been stymied by the accident. He was angry at Jeff for an earlier incident he'd later found out Jeff had had no part in. Ross had blamed the victim, saying that Jeff, as a professional rider, should have taken note of the condition of his own girth.

But now it all made sense. Jeff's accident hadn't been an accident at all. Neither Hope nor Jeff had been careless. Someone had deliberately destroyed that girth and set out to do serious harm to the rider.

A sinister thought occurred to Ross, sending his heart pounding. What about all the other accidents? Everyone, himself included, had chalked them all up to carelessness on the part of his men. But all but a few of these men had been with him for years, and the others had come highly recommended.

The only thing that made sense, as he sat there staring at a piece of rotted leather, was that someone was out to get not only Laurel Glen but him. For no one had known that Jeff would ride Ross's Prize that day or that Hope would, out of habit, grab Ross's tack to saddle the horse. As he recalled one incident after another, they all added up to sabotage.

But who? And why?

He thought back to the first crazy accident. It had been a couple weeks before Jeff's accident. A fence bordering the main road had been hit by a car or small truck in the middle of the night and had gone unnoticed till a neighbor found a horse, usually boarded at Laurel Glen, wandering on Indian Creek Road.

Ross's stomach did a sickly flip, and he almost gagged. That had been two days after Cole came home to Laurel Glen. What had he himself said to Meg that morning? "Maybe he's just come home to punish me for Marley's death."

No! It had to be a coincidence. Cole might hate him but he would never destroy his own heritage or resort to hurting another living soul. Cole had been genuinely upset at the deaths of those kittens and cats earlier. And the day that hay stack had tipped, Cole hadn't been anywhere near the debacle.

But that could have been a real accident, a silent voice accused.

No! His heart—his soul—rebelled. It couldn't be Cole. He refused to even go there!

But he had to do something. All he held dear was under attack, and the person responsible had to be stopped. He knew also that in his hand was the proof that Jeff's accident had been attempted murder, even if the wrong person had been injured. He had no choice but to call the police. Before he could think of the ramifications to Laurel Glen, Ross pulled out his cell phone and made the call to the state police.

Amelia Howard checked her directions and turned onto Indian Creek Road. After that she made note of the number on her trip odometer so she would know when she'd driven the three miles to Laurel Glen's entrance. When she saw a lovely wooden sign with Lavender Hill Farm written in deeply routed gold lettering, she knew she was less than a mile away.

The next drive would be Laurel Glen's. A mile later she brought the car to a stop at the ornate iron entrance gate. Amelia sat transfixed by the beauty of the ironwork arch. The wrought iron had been worked into laurel flowers and broad leaves that twined through fragile-looking iron latticework. Before she realized what she was doing, Amelia was out of the car, her Nikon aimed at the archway. The fields spread out on either side of it. A ribbon of a road ran through it and wove on ahead and over a hill. Clustered along the sides of the road was mountain laurel, its shiny leaves glimmering in the sunshine.

When they bloom in spring it must be a magnificent sight, Amelia thought, especially the way the archway framed the home where it sat on a distant hill. Meg had called it Laurel House.

Fighting the urge to spend a roll of film then and

there, Amelia climbed back in her Jeep and put the transmission into drive. As she crested the hill, she saw what those in the main house would see from its shining windows. Lying between her and Laurel House was what Amelia was sure was the business end of Laurel Glen. The working buildings sat cozily in the hollow between the hill she'd just come over and the one Laurel House graced. The stone facade of Laurel House seemed to spring up from the hillside, an exquisite ingredient of the southern Pennsylvania landscape.

Four one-story stone buildings Amelia assumed were stables lay in an X pattern with a large circular paddock joining them in the center. Off to the left sat a vintage stone barn. All the rest of the land was crisscrossed with white fencing, open meadows and wide dirt pathways.

So this is Laurel Glen, she thought. She'd never been on a horse farm and she was curious. The place should have sounded like a foreign country to Amelia, but when Meg had described it, something warm had stirred within her. And even now that she was here it still struck a chord, and that chord said home.

Chapter Two

Telling herself she was being fanciful in thinking this was the place she had searched for the world over, Amelia drove on. Just as she passed the last stable building and drew even with the octagon-shaped barn, a tall man on a cell phone walked into the sunlight toward the house. Amelia pulled even with him at about the same moment he took the little phone from his ear and pushed a button on its face with his thumb.

Talk about scenery, Amelia thought, tempted to snap a few unauthorized pictures of this Eastern cowboy in the straw Western-style hat. He walked just the way the rodeo riders she'd photographed in the Southwest did. All loose-limbed and fluid. And, she told herself, he was probably just as undepend-able as those riders she'd interviewed.

"Hi, there," she said bringing the car to a stop.

"I seem to be headed your way. Can I give you a lift up to the house?"

The man stared at her for a long, uncomfortable moment and frowned, but even the unpleasant expression couldn't hide his dark good looks. The straw cowboy hat shaded his eyes, but their blue color couldn't be hidden, nor could the youthful glow of his skin. She knew he had to be an employee because he was too young to be the owner, Ross Taggert, and too old to be Meg's nephew, Cole.

"This is private property," Cowboy Hunk said, then demanded, "what are you doing wandering around?"

Nice-looking as he was, he was still rude and arrogant. Amelia added those typical male traits to undependable. "I'm not wandering," she said firmly. "I'm going to Laurel House to visit your boss."

The man smiled, and her heart thumped a little harder.

"Last I heard I didn't have a boss, unless of course you're talking about my sister, and she only *thinks* I do what she says."

So this was Ross, and he had a portrait aging for him in the attic, or it was the son, Cole, and he looked older than she'd expected. He stepped closer to the car and cocked his head as if waiting for the answer to a question. Unfortunately, if he was, the question had flown right out of her head.

"I'm here to visit Meg Taggert. My name is

Amelia Howard,'' she said, hoping that information would clear up any confusion.

His frown deepened even as knowledge dawned in his deep-blue eyes. ''Ah. The reporter.''

''Oh, no. I'm not a reporter. I haven't had an article in a newspaper since college. And the only magazines that publish my work are travel and in-flight magazines.''

Just then his cell phone rang. He looked at the phone then at her. ''I hope your timing gets better, Ms. Howard, because so far it's pretty bad. You'll have to go on up the house alone. Tell Meg for me… No, never mind. This better come from me.''

He turned half away, looking troubled and anxious. He put the phone to his ear, stuck his free hand in his back pocket and cocked his hip. Amelia didn't know what got into her but she brought her camera to her eye, focused and shot the picture.

Now she just had to find out which Taggert her Eastern cowboy was so she could label it right.

Moments later Amelia parked in the circular stone drive in front of Laurel House and got out, taking only her purse to the house. Three sets of stairs rose ahead of her. Each set had six steps and ended at a terrace, which led to the next set of stairs and another terrace beyond them. As Amelia approached the front door, Meg opened it and walked to her with her arms extended in welcome, one of her signature caftans flowing behind her. Amelia automatically smiled.

"Darling!" Meg said, giving Amelia a warm hug.

She hugged her new friend back. The odd feeling of homecoming Amelia had felt while driving onto the farm returned and strengthened.

"You made wonderful time," Meg went on as they stepped away from each other. "I had no idea you'd arrive so early. This is wonderful."

Amelia chuckled, thinking of the cowboy in the straw hat. At Meg's inquiring look Amelia shrugged. "I wasn't sure how wonderful being early was. I was just told by a tall, dark-haired grump in a white straw Stetson that I have bad timing. I feel like I should drive back to that little town I went though a few miles ago and kill a couple of hours."

"That brother of mine!" Meg fumed, then giggled like a schoolgirl discussing an annoying pest of a younger brother. "He is, as ever, the bane of my existence, whom I just happen to love to death."

"So it's the portrait," Amelia muttered, the question of the day finally answered.

"Portrait?"

"As in Dorian Gray. As young as you look, I should have been prepared."

"Ah, but I work at it. He just slathers on sunscreen in the morning and goes about his day. He could at least have the good grace to get a few gray hairs. But I can forgive him just about anything right now. Things aren't good for Ross these days."

"Is he taking your niece's marriage that hard?"

"Goodness, no. He's simply thrilled about Jeff joining the family."

"But?" Amelia was confused. Last she'd heard, Ross Taggert hated the man her daughter had fallen in love with.

Meg looked around as if suddenly aware of her surroundings. "Oh, where are my manners? Come into the house and we'll sit and I'll catch you up on everything I was in no mood to go into in depth on the cruise. I admit it's all a little confusing—even for me."

Meg led her along the terrace, past a profusion of flowers to a lovely sitting room at the back of the house. They entered by French doors into a sanctuary that reminded Amelia of her grandparents' sun porch. It was decorated with white wicker furniture, rattan tables and lattice accents. The cushions on the settee and chairs were a cheery yellow and white. The out-of-doors followed them inside with a profusion of green plants that grew everywhere. The tall windows overlooked more fenced pastures, fields tall with corn and a distant tree line.

After Meg used an intercom to ask someone named Ruth Ann to bring them iced tea and a snack, Amelia asked about the view. She learned from Meg that the pastures and the cornfields belonged to Laurel Glen and that the corn would be used for feed. The tree line formed the western boarder of Laurel Glen. She imagined the land, only a little over an hour from a major metropolitan area, would be worth a fortune.

"But enough about the operation here," Meg said. "We talked so much about your book idea on the phone that I didn't catch you up on what's been happening here. You'll need a bit of background, too." She smiled, a delightful sparkle in her pale blue eyes.

"So tell me before I say the wrong thing. Your brother already doesn't seem too happy to have me here. I could always stay at a motel," Amelia added uncertainly.

"You will do no such thing." Meg looked toward the clatter from beyond the doorway. "Ah, here are our refreshments. Ruth Ann is our diva of the kitchen. Ruth Ann, this is my friend Amelia Howard, from the cruise."

"Pleased to meet you, Ms. Howard," Ruth Ann replied with a cheery grin.

Amelia smiled at the small fireplug of a woman as she came forward with her tray.

"Ruth Ann, I can always count on you. This looks lovely," Meg said as her kitchen diva set down the shiny white tray. There were four tall frosty glasses of iced tea—a lemon wedge decorated each glass. A yellow checked dish covered with a white paper doily was heaped with plump blueberry muffins, and matching dishes were piled in the remaining space. Either they were expecting company or Ruth Ann thought Amelia could eat enough for a small battalion.

When Ruth Ann had gone, Meg got right down to her story. Her tone serious, she began. "As boys, Jeff, Hope's new husband, and our Cole were best friends even though Jeff was two years ahead in school. He was here almost more than he was home so Ross was nearly as close to Jeff as he was to Cole. Closer certainly than Jeff was to his own father."

Meg filled her in on the story of how Marley Taggert died when Ross tried to cajole Cole back onto a horse after he was thrown. Ross's wife had stepped in and was killed when she rode the horse to show Cole it was safe. Cole blamed Ross, and their relationship fell apart. That's when he started getting into trouble. Finally, a little over a year after his mother's death, Cole stole a police cruiser and went for a joyride—sirens and lights blaring.

"If that wasn't a plea for help, I've never heard one," Amelia said, recognizing the adolescent cry for help from her training in psychology.

"I thought so, too," Meg said on a sigh. "However, the police took a dim view of the incident. They caught up with him, and he was arrested. They also saw someone running away from the car when they got close. Cole said he'd been alone and refused to say who had been with him or to admit the officer was right. He still claims he was alone. Ross worked a deal with the judge and DA to send Cole to a military school in exchange for charges being dropped. Cole was furious. He swore he'd never come back, and he didn't until…''

"Until just before all the tension here sent you on the cruise where we met," Amelia filled in.

Meg nodded. "Exactly."

"You mentioned that your brother and his son don't get along, but I thought you said Ross was also beginning to alienate his daughter because of her feelings for Jeff."

"Well, that's an aside to the story of Cole's arrest. Addison Carrington, Jeff's father, was terribly jealous of Jeff's relationship with Ross. He came to Ross after Jeff went back to college and after Cole had been sent away in disgrace. He said he believed it had been Jeff who was with Cole that night. Ross was furious. At eighteen Jeff appeared to get away with what would have been a felony while Ross lost any chance of repairing his relationship with Cole. Then, after years of remaining friends in spite of Ross's objections, Hope fell in love with Jeff."

Amelia remembered this part of the tale. "But then Jeff pushed Hope away because he was crippled in the riding accident and Hope moved to Lavender Hill, determined to help him anyway. Ross must have been incredibly frustrated to lose a second child to Jeff."

"Yes, but while I was away, Jeff approached Ross and they all finally talked. Piecing things together, they realized that Addison had lied to destroy

Jeff and Ross's relationship. Ross had already begun to see Jeff in a new light, so, with the lie exposed for what it was, things got much better between Ross, Hope and Jeff.''

"That's wonderful."

Meg smiled, her eyes suddenly alight with good cheer. "What is really wonderful is what happened in church at the wedding yesterday. Jeff surprised us all by walking up the aisle to meet Hope. He still gets tired easily, but otherwise he's completely recovered."

"So, if all that is settled, what has your brother so uptight?" Amelia asked.

Ross leaned his shoulder against the doorjamb of the sitting room. He hadn't known he was quite so transparent, but the proof was in the snippet of conversation he'd just overheard. He took a few seconds before making his presence known and studied Amelia Howard.

She was pretty in a casual sort of way, he decided. The first thing he'd noticed about her, after her soft Southern accent, was her high cheekbones. Next, rather inappropriately, was that her wide, tapered lips looked perfect for kissing. He'd forced his eyes upward and away from dangerous territory. Her straight nose had a slight flare and was the perfect size for her slightly square face. Then he'd moved on to encounter eyes the color of the sky before a fall thunderstorm. It had been a scary few moments standing there in the drive nearly mesmerized by her mere presence.

She ran her fingers through her hair. It was styled carelessly, brushed off her face as if combing it had been an afterthought. It still framed her face as if she'd worked at it for hours, though. Sitting where she was with the sun shining on her loose curls, he noticed that the color nearly defied description. It wasn't any one defined shade but rather a mix of strands of bronzy gold, copper and blond set against a background color of rich, warm brown.

All in all, Amelia Howard was one very attractive distraction that he just didn't need underfoot right then. But from the part of the conversation he'd heard, he gathered she'd gotten that point. He hadn't meant to be rude but it must have seemed exactly like it to her. He just didn't want anyone else getting hurt.

"Things around the farm have been unsettled lately," Meg answered, more or less defending his behavior.

"And it's about to get even worse," he said by way of letting them know he was there. Both women looked over. Meg smiled. Amelia blushed, which took Ross by surprise. Most of the women of his acquaintance were too sophisticated and worldly to allow themselves to feel even slightly embarrassed about anything. Ross hated to admit it, but that sort of honest vulnerability was something he missed seeing in women. It only followed that Amelia would have it—whatever it was—in spades!

"I assure you," she said, quickly regaining her composure. "I do not spread rumors or carry tales. I'm here to take interesting and appealing pictures, find out about your ancestors and give a short account of where your family is today."

Thinking of the police detective on his way to the house at any minute, Ross grimaced. "Well, right now my family seems to be under attack."

Meg sat forward. "Ross?"

"Sorry, Meg, but that's the way it looks. Have you seen Cole today? I wanted to be able to tell him what's going on before he hears it from someone else."

"Before he hears what from someone else?" Meg demanded.

Ross swallowed and glanced at Ms. Howard. "Your houseguest may want to stay elsewhere once she hears this. Most, if not all, of the accidents we've been experiencing around here weren't accidents at all. Jeff's included."

Meg gasped and set her tea down with a shaking hand. "Why would anyone want to hurt Jeff?"

"Since it was my saddle, the police think it's a safe bet I was the target and not Jeff. Of course, since it's pretty well known that I rarely wear a helmet when I ride, and considering how severe Jeff's injuries were, they're calling it attempted murder. Now we just have to find out who did it."

"Did what?" Meg demanded.

"Poured a chemical on the girth where it broke. I came across it today in a box of spare parts. It had continued to rot and even affected the things around it. The police lab has it now."

"Are you sure?" Amelia asked, unable to resist. She might not be a reporter, but she did have a natural curiosity where mysteries were concerned.

"It sure didn't smell like leather," Ross told her.

"No, I meant, are you sure it wasn't accidental?"

Ross stuffed his hands in his back pockets and shook his head. "We keep the insecticides and herbicides locked up so accidents can't happen. There's just no reason or excuse for a caustic chemical to be near the tack."

"What would a chemical be doing near the tack room?" Cole asked, surprising Ross as much as his appearance had the women. He turned to the doorway he'd just entered through and stared at Cole. He's innocent, Ross avowed silently. I know he is.

"Cole, dear," Meg called and put her hand out.

Cole walked forward and took Meg's hand. "Hi, Aunt Meg. Who is this lovely lady?" he asked easily as if he met women like Amelia Howard every day. Ross figured as nice-looking a man as his son was, maybe he did.

"This lovely lady is my friend Amelia Howard," Meg said, smiling at Cole as if their world wasn't exploding all around them. "She's doing a book on our county and its founding families. She'll be staying with us for a while.''

Reaching out to take Amelia's hand with the one that was still free, Cole grinned. ''You've made my day, Ms. Howard. I rarely get to hold hands with one beautiful lady, let alone two at the same time. It is a pleasure to meet you. If you need anything, just let me know.''

Ross couldn't have been more surprised if a meteor had rained down on the room. Watching Cole charm the women, he felt a twinge of something he'd always considered an appalling trait. He was jealous. What was wrong with him? First he'd freely admitted to himself that Amelia Howard was pretty and attractive. He'd actually entertained the thought, if only for a second, of how her lips would feel under his. Now he, who didn't notice women, was jealous of his own son's ease in charming her.

Ross focused on Cole when his son said, ''Ruth Ann said you were looking for me, Dad. You look like you lost your last friend.''

Chapter Three

Ross blinked away errant thoughts and dragged himself back to the important subject at hand. "I lost *something*. I'm just not sure what yet. Maybe my mind," he muttered. "Why don't you sit down? I wanted to warn you of what's going on."

Cole sat next to Amelia, leaving the unoccupied wicker chair for him. Ross gritted his teeth, trying to ignore what felt like the urge to defend his territory. This is ridiculous! I just met the woman.

"I found something disturbing after you left," Ross began, forcing all other thoughts from his mind.

"And you wanted to warn me about it?" Cole asked, his deep brown eyes grave.

Ross nodded. "It looks as if Jeff's accident wasn't an accident at all. The girth responsible for his fall is on its way to the state police lab. When I came across it earlier there was a chemical smell to it, and it had continued to rot in the box. I think, and more important, the police think, that it was deliberately tampered with. The detective is calling it attempted murder.''

"Who would want to hurt Jeff?" Cole asked.

"Not Jeff. Me. It was my saddle, remember. Why would anyone assume Jeff would ride my horse or use my saddle? Hope said it was a last-minute decision and Jeff made the final choice of which horse he'd ride. It could just as easily have been Hope thrown that day.''

"Okay. Who would want to hurt *you?*" Cole asked.

"How about *you?*" Detective Lovell accused as he walked in. His sudden entry brought with it a threat, and the room took on a distinctive chill.

"That's uncalled for, Detective," Ross snapped, standing to face the detective.

"Are you going to tell me that for even one second you didn't think your son's appearance just before the first accident was suspicious?"

Ross glanced at Cole then away. "Laurel Glen is as much Cole's heritage as it is mine."

"You think I'd try to kill you?" Cole asked, hurt rife in his voice.

"No, I do not," Ross replied. "Don't let this idiot get to you."

Lovell crossed his arms. "That's funny. From what I understand, you two haven't gotten along in years, and he turned his back on his heritage years ago. I also hear that your son has an expunged record.''

"Juvenile records are supposed to be wiped clean,'' Ross countered.

"I thought you wanted these crimes solved, but now I find out that you lied to me, Taggert. I asked if anyone had a reason to be after you. You left out that your son threatened you before you shipped him off.''

"I didn't lie. That was thirteen years ago. My son and I may have a strained relationship but he wouldn't harm me or anyone else.''

"You want to comment on that?'' the detective asked Cole.

"You're doing such a bang-up job, why should I tread on your act? You really ought to take it on the road.''

Ross turned to look at Cole. It was as if his son had just lost ten years of hard-earned maturity. He was again the smart-mouthed, slouching adolescent who'd driven them all so crazy following Marley's death.

It's a defense mechanism!

Just like learning Jeff had been with his tutor when Cole stole the police cruiser, another whole chapter of history rewrote itself in a nanosecond.

"Detective, it is *not* open season on my son. Yes, Cole got into some trouble as a kid. It was nothing serious. Just a stupid prank. He is now a respected veterinarian. This is a blind alley. It isn't going to take you anywhere. I suggest you take your investigation in another direction.''

''I'll take my investigation where it goes. I want to know your whereabouts this morning, Dr. Taggert.''

''I told you Cole hasn't—''

''It's okay, Dad. I'm capable of answering without incriminating myself. I went to see Doc Brennan out on Route One about buying him out of his practice, Detective. Then I came home and found out about the kittens. That was about noon. Then one of the men brought the stricken older cats to me. I realized then what was wrong with them and sent someone looking for the antifreeze.''

''Thanks to Cole, we found it in time to save several horses,'' Ross said.

''How convenient that you could appear to be the hero of the hour,'' Lovell said. He turned and sauntered toward the door to the terrace. ''Oh, and, Dr. Taggert, don't leave town,'' he said, leaving by the outside door and leaving a deadly silence in his wake.

Amelia watched Ross struggle for something to say to Cole as the detective sauntered onto the terrace. But it was his son who took the floor.

''You thought I'd try to *kill* you?'' he asked, incredulous.

''No. I said I didn't,'' Ross told his angry son.

"You heard me tell him you would never do something like that."

"Yeah, I heard what you *said*. I also saw the truth on your face. When you realized someone had tried to kill you, your first suspect was me."

Amelia heard the hurt in Cole's voice even though he spoke in an angry tone. However, Ross reacted solely to the anger.

"What would you think? You left here swearing to kill me if you ever saw me again. Then two days after you returned, the accidents started. For a split second, when I realized what's been going on, I thought maybe you were the one responsible. But I dismissed the idea just as quickly. You've come too far in your life to risk losing everything for revenge. Old revenge, at that."

"Gee, Dad, glad to hear that you've noticed how very grown-up I am. Too bad you haven't noticed a few other things. Like that I have principles. Like I wouldn't hurt anyone unless it was to defend someone." He looked at his watch. "Well, would you look at the time. I really have to be going. Sorry to break up this happy little family meeting but I must have a patient waiting out there somewhere."

"Cole, sit back down and listen to me!" Ross demanded.

"No. I don't want to listen. And I'm too old to order around. I thought we'd established that you've realized that much about me." Cole turned and stormed out the same door the detective had used.

Having witnessed the entire scene, Meg sighed. "That went well," she said, her tone droll and disgusted at once.

"I told him I didn't suspect him."

Amelia watched Meg marshal herself for a battle that she plainly didn't intend to back away from. "Ross, you told your son you thought he was capable of murder. If only for a second, that *is* what you thought. That's exactly what he heard."

"No. I thought he might still want me dead, and he has good reason, but when I thought of someone actually doing each of the things that have set up these accidents, I knew it couldn't be Cole. Someone left antifreeze where the animals could get to it. Cole wouldn't hurt an animal."

"But he could want his father dead? Listen to yourself. Why would you think he'd value the life of an animal over yours?"

Ross stood. And when he opened his mouth, he sounded just like his son. "Gee, I don't know, Meg. Maybe because I killed his mother." It was Ross's turn to storm out, but he went through the house.

"That was special," Meg said, looking at Amelia. "I'm so sorry, Amelia. What an introduction to our family!"

"It's okay. My own family was stormy at times. We probably had problems opposite of yours, though. An older parent who couldn't seem to let me go. In this case, it's a younger parent who let go too soon."

"You should have been a psychologist."

Amelia shrugged, still a little uncomfortable with a degree she hadn't been able to put to use. "As a writer, I'm something of a student of human nature."

"At least you won't be bored around here. We've given you quite a bit to study already. So, as a disinterested observer, what did you see?"

Maybe she could help Meg's family and not get all wrapped up in the undercurrent of emotions the way she had during her aborted internship. Maybe all the money her parents had spent on a degree she didn't have the desire to use wouldn't go to waste, after all.

"Ross and Cole clearly love each other," she said after some thought. "Ross wants desperately to be a father to his son, and Cole wants his father's approval in the worst way, which in essence proves he wants Ross to act like a father."

"Too true. And neither will accept what they need from the other. It's been like this since Cole came back. They slid into familiar patterns within days of Cole's return."

"There's another thing, as well. Cole blames Ross for his mother's death. So does Ross, obviously. But do they ever talk about it?"

"Absolutely not. Mention Marley's name near either of them, and the temperature in the room drops into the arctic zone. I don't believe in ghosts, but her memory haunts this place just the same."

"Ross must have loved her very much."

"And I've never figured out why. She was none of the things Ross was raised to value or that he seems to value now. Yet he can't forget her. He hasn't gone on even one date in all these years. As close as he's come is to dance with the women who attend the big Valentine's party that's held here every year. And then he's only doing it as a part of the duty of being the host."

Amelia sighed and sat back, trying to relax. That had been one of the more tense scenes she'd witnessed since she and her mother used to go at it years ago. She felt the need to change the subject.

"That's sad, although truthfully, Ross's love life doesn't sound all that different from mine."

"I didn't notice you shying away from all that male attention on the ship."

"No. I haven't closed myself off to the idea of romance and eventually marriage, but my standards are a little rigid for today's men."

"What are they?"

"I'd like someone dependable. A strong man the way my father was strong. A man interested in family and God more than he's interested in money, his career and having a good time. He just isn't out there, I'm afraid. And I won't settle for less than the kind of man the Lord would have me take to my heart."

"Well, good for you. Too bad Ross is so anti-

God, or you'd have just described my handsome little brother."

Amelia sent her a wry look. "You left out that he's still in love with his wife. Did I mention needing to be second only to the Lord in a man's life?"

"You didn't have to. I know what that feels like."

Meg's wistful tone alerted Amelia to another interesting story. "Who was *your* Mr. Right and what happened to keep you from getting married?"

"His name was Wade Jackson." Meg smiled wistfully. "We met in New York when he was there on leave. It was a wonderful whirlwind romance, and we were engaged by the time his month of leave was over." She put her tea down, hesitated then continued. "Wade was a pilot, and what got in the way was a little police action in the sixties called Vietnam."

The grief was still so thick in Meg's tone that guessing the rest was easy. "Oh. He was killed, wasn't he?"

Meg bit her lip and blinked away tears. "It was the emptiest time of my life, but it brought me the greatest joy in the long run. I found the Lord as a result of our relationship, and He got me through the rest. We, Ross and I, were raised in the church, but what our minister said about the Lord never clicked with me back then. For a while I thought it had with Ross but then I heard he'd married Marley and I knew it was only wishful thinking on my father's part.''

Meg looked at her elegant watch, clearly uncomfortable with the turn of the conversation. ''Goodness, as Cole would say, look at the time. We need to get you settled and leave some time for you to rest before dinner. I'm afraid meals around here are every bit as exciting as snack time was. You're sure you wouldn't rather stay with Hope and Jeff when they get back?''

''Nonsense. I came here to see you. The research for the book was only an excuse. Remember?''

Amelia hung up the last of her clothes and shut the door of the armoire. Her room had the same beautiful view as the little room off the terrace where they'd had tea. She walked to the window and saw someone riding in the distance. She remembered what Ross had said about not wearing one of those little velvet-covered riding helmets when he rode. So the person in the distance, wearing a straw cowboy hat and jumping fences on a majestic black horse, must be Ross.

Goodness, he was attractive. And he was, as Meg had pointed out, exactly the kind of man Amelia had hoped to meet one day. He was a man in the true sense of the word. He was strong but not afraid to admit his love for his children, his land or his heritage. He understood the concepts of truth, honor and commitment.

And now that she understood all the pressure he'd come under earlier in the day, she could easily forgive his rudeness. *"I hope your timing gets better, Ms. Howard, because so far it's pretty bad."* Amelia chuckled as his words replayed themselves in her head. He must have been terribly frustrated with her.

Watching him out there, putting that huge black beast through his paces, made her heart race. He was a magnificent sight. Amelia reached for her camera on instinct alone. She needed to make a permanent record of this memory.

Several minutes later, she sat perched on a pasture fence using her telephoto to capture images of a sport she saw as a curious balance of wildness and discipline. Ross was clearly a talented rider. He and the black horse seemed to float over the barriers no matter how high, wide or complicated. After two rolls of film, she finally stopped holding her breath as they approached each fence, hedge or water hazard.

Amelia was busy changing to her fourth roll when the pounding of hooves and the creak and jingle of tack alerted her to Ross's approach. Looking up, she lofted her camera to shoot him as he approached, then Amelia focused the lens. His handsome face had her holding her breath all over again. Her stomach did a little elevator-ride flip. She was too well trained to miss the shot, however. Or the next when his lips tipped up in a heart-stopping smile.

"Now there's a waste of film if I ever saw one,"

he said as he swung his leg over the saddle and dropped to the ground.

Amelia brought her camera down to rest on one bent leg. "No film is ever wasted. The best picture I ever took was an accidental double exposure." Ross's crooked eyebrow seemed to ask an explanation so she gave one. "I was shooting in the Smokey Mountains and I'd just taken a shot of a sheer, snow-dappled cliff face. An old man, leading what had to be an even older donkey, walked into the meadow below the cliff. I was so distracted by the sudden appearance of another person so far from civilization that I shot him using the same camera. Then I remembered that I hadn't advanced the film after the shot before. I reshot him, then the cliff again, but neither print was as good as that accidental first one. I won an award for it."

"Were you all alone out there in the mountains? The Smokeys can be some rough terrain."

"No. I had a guide. I have a healthy fear of nature and the elements, believe me. My first wilderness shoot was as a last-minute replacement for some guy who must have thought he was Tarzan or something. Apparently he broke his leg when he fell off a cliff he didn't notice in time. I hired a guide and always have since, even in metropolitan areas."

Ross chuckled, and the sound played along her spine, raising the fine hairs on her arms. This man was dangerous!

"You didn't have one earlier, and you encountered a bear as soon as you arrived," he quipped.

Amelia nodded sagely. "Hmm. *Ursidae Chester Countes.* I've heard from informed sources that his growl is worse than his bite. I'm not about to hear differently, am I?"

Ross knocked the hat back on his head, unshading his incredible sapphire eyes and smiled widely. "No, ma'am. Especially since Sally and Ruth Ann have joined your fan club. Meg alone is scary enough. I'd be crazy to take on all three."

"And why would you want to?" she asked seriously.

"Because right now I don't have a lot of time to baby-sit a houseguest, no matter how world traveled she may be."

Amelia jumped to the ground. At five foot seven, she rarely had to tilt her head to look someone in the eye. Standing in front of Ross Taggert, she had to do just that. Though it put her at a disadvantage in their current discussion, she had to admit the feeling appealed to some illogical streak in her. Maybe it was female intuition that told her he would never use his superior size for any reason but to protect.

"I hardly require a baby-sitter," she told him, doing her best to stand tall and look him in those impossibly blue eyes. "Last birthday I seem to remember having earned thirty-seven candles." Amelia didn't add that she'd been in the Hawaiian rain forest at the time and had toasted her thirty-seventh year with some purified water in the company of a stranger whom she'd hired as a guide.

"Maybe I should have said guard," Ross corrected. "Whatever word you choose, if you get hurt while you're staying here, I'm going to feel responsible. I don't like the feeling or need the worry."

"I promise to be careful, Ross. I'm not a fool. Meg said she has boxes of old photos for me to go through. I can stay close to the house and pick out the photos I want to use with comparison shots. That could take as long as a week. When I'm ready to do the comparison shots, I'll go get the photos I need elsewhere before I do the ones of Laurel Glen. That would give the police time to discover who has it in for you."

Ross sighed and rubbed the back of his neck. "I'd appreciate it. But even at that, don't go anywhere outside the house without letting Cole or me know about it."

Glad he'd included Cole as a man she could trust, Amelia nodded and put her camera strap over her head. "Then that's how we'll handle things. I do thank you for letting me stay here. Meg and I really hit it off on the cruise, and I'd like the chance to get to know her better. This was supposed to be a working vacation for me."

"Which is why no guide?"

She couldn't help it. Her lips tipped up, and she smirked at him. "Actually, Meg promised to provide a guide. You."

Chapter Four

Ross picked himself up, dusted himself off and ambled toward the edge of the ring. He looked at the three-year-old gelding he'd been working with and glowered as he led him along. "Make sure Ice Cream gets a nice bath. Maybe that'll relax him," he said to Harry Donovan, then chuckled, his good nature rising above his annoyance over getting dumped. "Ice Cream. Where do they get these names?"

"If I remember right, the mother said when they gave him to their kid, he asked why he hadn't gotten ice cream for his birthday like all his other friends. Guess that's what they get for giving a four-year-old a colt he couldn't ride. Crazy yuppies. Got more money than brains. Wonder if the kid even remembers old Ice Cream here exists anymore."

Ross gave the bay American Saddlebred a pat on

the rump and loosened the girth of the saddle. "Well, whatever their intentions were, Ice Cream here will be a fine show horse if I can get him to stop shying at jumps."

"Did that hurt?" a feminine voice asked from beyond the ring's fence.

Ross turned toward Amelia and walked over to her. "Only my pride." He looked around. She was alone. "You aren't supposed to go anywhere without Cole or me."

She pointed to the doorway of the stable to her right where Cole knelt, checking the forelock of a black Welsh Cob Pony that had been Cole's first horse. He was the pony who had carried both his kids as toddlers.

"They asked him to look at that little horse. Cobby, I think. He's so little and cute compared to other horses. It would be kind of like buying a puppy who'll never grow up."

Ross chuckled, then opened the gate to the ring and stepped into the yard. "He'd be a lot harder to housebreak, and I'm afraid your carpets would never survive." She laughed, and his heart kicked a little in his chest. He actually reached up and rubbed the spot.

"I don't think the landlord would appreciate him, and neither would the neighbor under me. I imagine Cobby would be a little heavy footed." She frowned, staring at his hand over his heart. "Are you all right? You didn't hurt yourself did you?"

Aware suddenly of his actions, he dropped his hand and shoved it in his back pocket. "Me? Nah. I'm used to getting dumped. What, no camera to record my humiliation?" he asked smoothly, he hoped, changing the subject.

"No. I didn't know there'd be such a prime photo op or I would have brought it. I actually came looking for you because I have a favor to ask. Meg tells me a couple I'll want to interview are leaving for a trip to see their daughter in California the day after tomorrow. The Hansells. They said I could come over today but that getting to their place is complicated. Meg can't go. She has some sort of historical society meeting she has to attend. I wondered if you'd be free to go with me. I'd hate to get turned around on these back roads."

He thought about all he had to do that day, then glanced toward Cole. Cole could take her. He'd run with the Hansells' youngest son so he knew where their place was. Although Ross couldn't see anything developing between himself and Amelia, the idea of her with Cole annoyed him.

Okay. I'm being a dog in the manger. But I like her and I want to spend time with her. What's so wrong with that? I just want to get to know her better. As a person. And no one has to know but me that I'm this attracted to her. I'll just act friendly, and she won't get other ideas. Even Cole admitted that all he seems to do is hurt the women he gets involved with. So, in a way, I'd be protecting her.

"I can run you over there in about forty-five minutes."

Ross opened the door to his 4×4 and held Amelia's camera bag while she hopped up onto the high seat. She was digging the camera out before he closed the door, drawing a smile from Ross. She had so much enthusiasm. He'd noticed that about her during the first meal she ate with the family a little over two weeks ago. She asked questions about everything and listened to the answers. Really listened. Not like Marley, who he'd come to realize had asked questions then tuned out the answers their whole married life. She'd been all about show.

Marley had quite honestly snared him in senior year of high school and trapped him into marriage before the summer after graduation was gone. No one had ever known her or what she was thinking. Least of all him—her husband—who she managed to fool for years until it no longer suited her purpose.

It had been the mystery of her that drew him and the forbidden fruit of the richest girl in school wanting him that had slammed the door on the trap that became his life. He was still locked behind that door fourteen years after her death. It was no longer love but guilt that barred the door to freedom. Had he loved her so much that he'd killed her?

"What are the Hansells like?" Amelia asked, snapping Ross out of his reverie as he drove under Laurel Glen's entrance arch.

"Elderly," he said, then went on, his mind ordered in the present, his dark thoughts of the past tucked away again. "We were never friends. They're quite a bit older than I am. Actually, my parents were acquaintances of theirs. Georgina and Farrell's youngest and my oldest ran together, at least until Cole..." Ross hesitated. He didn't want to talk about Cole to Amelia. "Well, anyway, they were much older than we were."

"Is their place as changed from the old days as Laurel Glen?"

He shook his head and negotiated the truck onto the right fork in the road. "It's nearly identical to what it was two hundred years ago so it should be interesting to see those early photos next to yours. When I was a kid they still had a painting of the place that was done by the wife of the man who was given the original land grant by William Penn. I'll bet if they still have it they'll let you take a close-up of it. You can do that, can't you?" Ross asked as he put his turn signal on and turned onto the main road.

"I've taken the photos for several catalogues for art galleries and auction houses. It shouldn't be a problem unless it's badly darkened, which can happen with old oils. Is theirs a big farm?"

"It was, but they've sold off most of the acreage to a developer. They only kept the five acres surrounding them. That was about five years ago, when Farrell decided it was time to retire the tractor and himself. I imagine the rest will go after their deaths. Their son is an aerospace engineer in Houston, and their four daughters have moved all over the country.''

''What a shame. But I guess you can't blame them. Farming seems to be a dying industry around the big eastern cities.''

''It's being killed. It isn't dying. But I don't want to get into that. My blood pressure can't take it.''

He felt her turn toward him. ''Are you having problems?''

Ross winced. How had he let that slip? It was a good thing she wasn't a reporter. No one would be safe around her. She'd get her subject talking, and they'd tell all without knowing what hit them. ''I'm healthy as a horse,'' he said, evading the question. ''So what got you into photography?''

''A little cartridge-film camera for my tenth birthday. By the time I reached sixteen, I had a cheap thirty-five millimeter and I was working part-time to pay for developing. My mother didn't appreciate my talent then. She saw it as a waste of money and a corrupting influence.''

''So, did you go to school for it?''

''Eventually,'' she said, her voice a little tight.

Ross took his eyes off the straight road to glance at her. She looked as if a faraway, bad memory had surfaced. He wanted to ask, but he had his secrets and he wasn't willing to share them. It wouldn't be fair to pry into hers.

"Am I completely out of the loop or is it okay that I don't recognize your name?" he asked.

She laughed. It was a lively, lovely sound, and he felt his heart trip once again. This time he studiously ignored it. He had to. The most they could be was friends, and he had to get a handle on his reaction to everything about her. Marley was dead, robbed of the happiness she'd planned for her life because of him. He had no right to find love again.

"I've done some calendar work but I've noticed the calendars at Laurel Glen have a decidedly equestrian theme. There are some obscure art galleries here or there across the country with my work, too. The only other way you would know me would be if you were the type to haunt your local bookstore for coffee table pictorials."

Ross glanced at her again and found her giving him a long look. When their eyes met she grinned. "You don't look like the sedentary type to me. But then again there are two books of mine in the sunroom."

"That's Meg's room," he said, but thought he might take the time to go hunting for them in there later. Just to see if her work reflected what he'd learned about her so far.

"It looks like Meg decorated, doesn't it? I was sure you didn't have a hand in the decorating, except to provide the wherewithal, that is. Meg grumbled about not being allowed to pay for the changes she made."

Ross frowned. "She's contributed plenty. She was a mother to Hope. And she shouldn't spend what little is hers on a house she won't be passing on to her children."

"That bothers you." It wasn't a question.

His frown tensed into a full-fledged scowl. "Of course it bothers me. I tried to give her half what Laurel Glen was worth several years ago but she wouldn't take it. She said she'd leave if I brought it up again. This is her home. All her friends are here. So I keep my mouth shut and write checks."

"I wouldn't have taken what you've earned, either. From what Meg says, if you hadn't worked day and night, Laurel Glen might have gone to pay taxes."

That was true. But his father had been wrong to leave Meg out of the will because she wanted to be an actress. With the exception of leaving the rental property to Meg, Ross had split everything equally in his own will between his children in spite of the bad blood between him and Cole. Laurel Glen was their birthright. Personality conflicts had no place in that.

"Even back then, it would have been worth a few million," he told Amelia. "More after, but by then Laurel Glen was pretty well established again, and the loan I had to take out to pay the estate taxes was paid off."

"After? After what?"

He grimaced again and sighed inwardly. Why did

she have to notice one little word in the midst of all those others he'd uttered? And how did she drag this stuff out of him? Even more important, why did he feel compelled to answer?

"Marley was an only child. Her parents had just died months apart, and she'd inherited their entire estate. When she was killed about six months later, I was her sole heir."

"And the money allowed you to upgrade Laurel Glen?"

"No, her parents owned the farm next to ours, but theirs wasn't a working farm. Just a lot of acreage they paid to have mowed occasionally and a small stable for their personal mounts. Marley was an event rider with a pretty high ranking. They had always been way out of our family's league financially. I paid the estate tax out of their assets and put the rest of the money in trusts for Cole and Hope."

"I thought Lavender Hill was your nearest neighbor."

"This was on the western side of us. And the house was set at the farthest border of their property. I rent it and a few acres around it to corporate executives who don't stay in one place too long. They can afford a big place like that but don't want the burden of ownership. We incorporated the rest of the land in with Laurel Glen's. That house is the rental property I mentioned that I plan to leave to Meg."

"Were either of Marley's parents descendants of founding fathers?"

Ross thought back. "No... It seems to me they bought the place from the original family when Marley was in first grade. She went to a private school till high school but she took lessons at Laurel Glen."

"You married your childhood sweetheart?"

"Not really. She didn't notice me till high school. But then again we were children when we married. Does that count?" He forced a smile he didn't feel. Every time he thought of those days with his more mature mind, he wanted to cringe. He'd been so enamored that he'd never seen the real Marley. The spoiled, pouting, faithless person beneath the perfect exterior she'd shown the world, her children and even him. She'd been a chameleon, and being handed her parents' wealth had revealed the beautiful camouflage for what it was. A facade. A life that was a lie.

Amelia saw the pain and discomfort speaking of Marley caused him in every line of his body. Amelia was sorry that she'd tried to get him to talk about her. They'd been having such a nice chat. At first she'd been able to imagine a young Ross making goo-goo eyes at the little girl next door when she came for lessons, but then he'd gotten all tense and uptight. She noticed that he wasn't cold, the way Meg described his reaction to any mention of his late wife, but he did seem angry—heatedly so. She thought this anger might be more healthy for him emotionally, but his casual mention of his blood pressure made her wary of the effect on his physical health.

Quickly, trying to slide off the subject of Marley Taggert and on to her project, Amelia said, "I'll have to research the original family. Since we know the end of their story it would be great to discover and use the beginning. It's an approach I hadn't thought of. Do you think the current renters would mind my taking some shots of the house and the outbuildings?"

Ross shrugged. "I'll call them and ask. All they can say is no, but I doubt they will."

"That's sweet of you."

For some reason he thought her compliment was funny. He laughed, the sound filling the air-conditioned 4×4 cab.

"What?" she demanded.

He shot her a crooked grin then looked at the road, slowing down and flipping on his turn signal. "No one has ever called me sweet," he told her. "My daughter, Hope, is sweet. Candy is sweet. I thought we'd established me as the beast of Laurel Glen. *Ursidae Chester Countes,* wasn't it?"

"Ah, but that was before I got to know you better. In the last two weeks I've discovered that not only is your bark worse than your bite, but you've got no bite at all where family and friends are concerned. You're all growl and no action."

"Are you sure you didn't come here looking to destroy my hard-earned rep as a tough guy?"

"Tough guy? Those kids you teach have you wrapped around their little fingers. And they bring you presents. You must have been a terrific father. Look at the wonderful children you raised. A son who was given the Golden Eagle by the Equine Surgery Association for an innovative surgical technique, and a daughter who's at the top of her field at the age of twenty-seven."

"Don't applaud too soon. Hope got where she is by leaving Laurel Glen to work elsewhere. I was so afraid to let her close to the animals without me or our retiring trainer watching her every second that I refused to give her the job she deserved. It took me a year and a half to break down and swallow my pride and ask her to come home."

"She was how old?"

"Twenty-four. I'm a blind fool when it comes to my kids, not a good father at all."

"Hope was the person you made her, Ross. Just as I'm the person my parents made me. Nothing the world threw at me after age sixteen changed that. Take it from the daughter of a great father."

"Well, I sure don't deserve any credit where Cole is concerned. I haven't been a father to him since his fifteenth birthday."

"Do you want to talk about it?"

"Nah. What's the use? What's past is past. I can't go back and change my mistakes," he said, trying to sound as if it no longer mattered to him, but Amelia heard the pain in his voice as he flipped on his turn signal once again.

They turned down a narrow road that was no more than a tunnel through the dense umbrella of treetops. It was so deeply shadowed that the midday sun was all but blotted out. Amelia took off her sunglasses and turned away from the green blur of the lush undergrowth whizzing by. She longed to draw Ross out and help him see that it wasn't too late for him and his son. She told him just that.

"Yes, it is. He doesn't even bother to argue with me anymore. Detective Lovell helped me put the last nail in that coffin. I doubted Cole, and now he knows it."

"Maybe if you sat down with him and explained…" Amelia trailed off, seeing Ross shake his head.

"Haven't you noticed? The one thing we haven't been able to do in fourteen years is sit down and talk. Scream at each other? Retreat behind a wall of silence? Those things we're good at. But talk? Really talk? It doesn't work that way. Not between us."

"I'm sorry. From what I've seen, your son is a good man. You two are so much alike." She chuckled thinking of Ross's parting shot the day she'd arrived, when he'd stormed off and left her and Meg in the sunroom.

He glanced over, clearly perplexed by her reaction

to so serious a subject, his brows drawn together in a scowl. "What?"

"Sometimes you even sound alike."

His expression said she'd taken leave of her senses. "Huh?"

"When Detective Lovell cornered him, Cole transformed into a smart-mouthed teenager in the blink of an eye."

Ross nodded. "I finally figured out, watching him with someone else as the target, that it's a defense mechanism for Cole. But you're right. He lost a good number of years off his maturity scale in about two point two seconds."

She noticed he'd relaxed, so she went in for the kill. A professor had once said that you had to hit some people over the head with the truth. Ross was one of those people. "Glad you recognized it. Because so did you just minutes later."

"Me?"

Amelia chuckled at his incredulous tone. "Let's see. Meg asked why you would think Cole would care more about an animal than he did you. And you said, 'Gee, I don't know. Maybe because I killed his mother.' Believe me, you lost twenty years off *your* maturity scale. At first I thought you were doing an imitation of Cole, but then I realized it was more a case of like father like son. Smart mouth is a defense mechanism for both of you."

He slowed the truck to a stop, put the turn signal on but didn't make the turn onto the deserted road to the left. Instead he just stared at her. Before she lost her nerve under his penetrating gaze, Amelia rushed on. "You didn't kill his mother. Meg told me your wife interfered in a situation between you and Cole and was accidentally killed."

Fire not ice made his eyes suddenly glow in the shadowed interior. "Did she tell you it would have been Cole on the horse—Cole lying trampled next to the horse minutes later? I had to destroy that demon to keep him from pounding her into dust. And just minutes earlier I'd ordered Cole to get back on after he was thrown. Did she tell you, Ms. Howard, that my son tried to tell me the horse was dangerous but that I wouldn't listen? No. I see from the look on your face she left out a few pertinent facts. You see, I really *did* kill my wife."

Chapter Five

Amelia walked slowly down the sweeping staircase to the first-floor foyer. She rubbed her damp palms together and smoothed her skirt, nervous about the coming dinner. Ross hadn't spoken to her for the rest of the ride to the Hansells'. He'd shown a staid politeness while they were with the older couple, then he'd reverted to silence on the way home. After having developed so friendly a rapport with him, his coolness was nerve-racking. Everyone at the dinner table was sure to notice they'd had some sort of falling out.

Meg breezed into the foyer out of the dining room and smiled as Amelia descended the last step. "Don't you look pretty," she said.

"I'm still not used to dressing for dinner, but it has been a nice change," Amelia admitted as she fell in step with Meg. "Most of the time I grab a fast meal in a motel restaurant or eat around a campfire. When I'm home, I'm usually rushing to get business handled, so I eat at my computer or in front of the TV.''

"You need a life, girl!" Meg declared, shaking her head.

"You aren't telling me anything I don't know already. I keep meaning to ask how you managed to start this tradition with men and teenagers to contend with?"

"Our grandmother did all the work before Ross and I came along. She considered the kitchen and meals her domain while she was alive. Granny Taggert outlived our mother and Marley. No one showed up at Granny's table smelling like a horse." Meg laughed lightly. "Believe me. If you'd known my grandmother you'd understand.

"But enough about family history. Sit," Meg ordered, gesturing to the cream-colored country French sofas, which faced each other on either side of the fireplace. "Now, tell me what put the bee under my darling brother's bonnet?"

"I did. I think I stepped on his toes about his wife's death." Amelia grimaced and sank to the sofa, and Meg sat on the other. "No. I take that back. I know I did. Actually, I guess I stomped on them."

"Uh-oh. I did warn you."

"I didn't bring her name up. He more or less did. I just pointed out that saying he'd killed her was a little over the top and no less juvenile than Cole's attitude with that police detective the day he was here.''

Meg's eyes widened. "Double uh-oh. Amelia, what were you thinking?"

"I don't know. It's so sad to see him torturing himself and giving up on his relationship with Cole. He thinks there's no hope of salvaging things between them."

Meg stared at her. Worry creased her brow. "Oh, Amelia, honey, don't fall for my baby brother. You were right. You need someone who loves you, and I'm afraid, like me, my brother will only have one love in his lifetime."

Amelia wished she could assure her friend that she was missing the mark by a mile, but she couldn't. Ross's appeal grew each day she was there. Every time she witnessed him with a child or brooding over the farm or his relationship with Cole she could feel her heart expand, willing Ross closer. And all she had to do was see him—even at a distance—and her heart picked up its beat. She was well and truly on her way to caring deeply for a man who barely tolerated her.

"Ah. I've wandered into a paradise," Cole said as he walked in. "And the sweetest flowers seem to be mine for the taking."

Meg threw her nephew a sardonic look. "If that's your best pickup line, you were born thirty years too late and you must be a very lonely young man."

Cole threw back his head and laughed, dropping down next to Meg and wrapping his long arms around his aunt to give her an affectionate squeeze and a noisy kiss on the cheek. "Aunty Meg. The family ego builder at work again. What would we do without you?"

"You'd be even more incorrigible, you scamp!" Meg laughed, trying to wiggle out of his embrace.

"Incorrigible? You wound me. You truly do! What do you think, Miss Amelia," he asked in a subtle imitation of Amelia's Southern accent. "Am I right to be distressed by so great an affront?"

"I think, sir," Amelia answered in as thick an accent as she could manage, "that you are every bit as full of it as Laurel Glen's compost heap."

A snicker drifted into the room, and they all looked over to the doorway where Cole had left the pocket doors open to the foyer. Ross stood there, a wry grin in place. "It's nice to know there are at least two intelligent women left in the race who see through that boyish charm of his."

Cole stiffened, took his arm from around Meg and stood. "Well, I wouldn't want to inflict my boyish self on anyone, so I'll just toddle along and have dinner with a friend. Evening, everyone," he said and left, walking by Ross without even glancing his way.

The hopelessness in Ross's eyes was easy to see. "I was only kidding. I guess teasing him is out of the question, too."

Just as easy to read was the sympathy in Meg's Taggert blue eyes. "We know you were only trying to tease him. Try not to let his mood get to you. He's just a little sensitive to anything that could be construed as criticism from you."

"A little sensitive?" Ross asked.

"Okay, a lot, but you can't let it do more than guide you in your choice of words," Meg advised.

He looked at Amelia. "You're such a great student of human nature. What do you think I should have said?"

Amelia knew a trap when she saw one. Ross was clearly gunning for her. Should she decline to get involved? She thought for a long moment. Since when have you ever run from a fight?

"Hello might have been safe," she suggested after some thought. "But I doubt it. It was Cole who was wrong. If you'd said he shouldn't let us talk to him that way, I'll bet he would have gone on the defensive and made it sound as if you'd attacked us."

"Amen," Meg declared. "Let's go have a nice dinner then I'm taking Amelia to Wednesday evening services."

"Why don't you come?" Amelia asked Ross, thinking the Lord was the only thing that could offer him any solace at such a difficult time in his life.

"The one thing Cole and I agree on is church and God. If He's so almighty powerful, then why did He let that crazy horse kill Marley and shatter this family? And why isn't He stopping the person who's out to destroy us? We stand to lose the only thing this family has left. Laurel Glen.''

"God didn't kill Marley," Meg argued. "That horse did, and ultimately the man who sold him to you. He had to know how dangerous that animal was.''

"God still let it happen.'' Ross looked away from Meg and at Amelia. "What? Nothing to say all of a sudden?'' he challenged.

"You're absolutely right," she answered quickly. It was the truth. Why deny it? "God did let it happen.'' If she'd been trying to shock him, Amelia thought, she'd hit the mark. Silence reigned in the exquisite, monochromatic room. And Ross simply stared at her, not only dumbfounded but totally confused. It showed in his expression, his posture, even the way he'd dropped his hands at his sides.

"Why aren't you denying it?'' he demanded, frowning deeply. "Everyone else always has. Aren't you going to tell me it must have been her karma to die early or that she could just as easily have been hit by a bus or choked on a steak?''

"I don't believe in karma, and you know she could have died any number of ways. But think of this. When God created Adam, He wasn't building a puppet. If He didn't take a general hands-off approach, if He stepped in all the time to keep us from making mistakes, what would happen to our free will?''

Again silence fell over the room. Even Meg seemed speechless—waiting.

"We'd all be Pinocchio," Amelia said, answering her own question. "We'd be living in a happy, mechanical utopia where nothing ever went wrong but where we had no freedom to make our own decisions. Would you want to live that way?"

Ross found himself sinking down to sit next to Meg. He didn't know what to say. It had been a long time since he'd thought about anything to do with the Almighty—since he'd allowed his thoughts to stray in that direction. But it didn't take much consideration at all to admit she was right. He wouldn't want to give up his free will to be safe from life's pain. It would be like being a machine. A robot. Not life but existence.

Finally, blessed anger surged to his rescue. "God still could have let her live."

"Ross," Meg said sharply. "You asked the question. Don't attack a guest because you don't like her answer."

"No, it's all right," Amelia said, holding up her hand. "He *could* have let her live. True. When I get to meet Him, I'll ask Him why He didn't. Right after I ask why my brother had to die in a terrorist explosion in the Middle East before I could see him again and why my parents had to die one after another. *I'll* have a chance to ask, but *you* won't, Ross." Her voice seemed to catch, and she cleared her throat before going on in her quiet, smooth-as-satin voice. "You can be as mad at God as you want but you aren't hurting Him as much as you're hurting you. Because you live your life without His help and more important, you're not going to get into heaven without Him. So what is this fourteen-year-long temper tantrum really about? Who are you really out to punish?"

Ross could only stare at Amelia as she got up and walked out, leaving her soft-spoken challenge to echo endlessly in the room.

"Oh, dear," Meg said, Amelia's Southern accent seeming to be catching. "I do believe Teddy Roosevelt would have adored that woman. Talk about walking softly and carrying a big stick." Meg stood to leave. "I think it might be better to let us eat alone tonight, brother dear. I believe my houseguest is a bit upset with you."

He watched her go and realized that he'd been virtually uninvited to his own dinner table. Before he could get angry, though, he realized he was relieved. There had been tears in Amelia's eyes when she'd left. Real tears. Tears for him. They hadn't been the crocodile kind Marley had scared up at the drop of a hat. Now that he saw real sadness in the eyes of a woman he cared for, it was easy to identify the other kind.

Cared for? Had that thought come from his brain? His heart? She was a nice lady, he told himself. Of course he cared that he'd made her cry. He hadn't meant to. He wasn't an ogre, after all. But that was all it was. Just regret. He cared *about* her, not *for* her. There was a huge difference.

Frowning, he got up and headed to the stables to check that the last of the day's chores had been properly handled before the men had gone home. He didn't usually go back after getting cleaned up for dinner, but considering the way things had been going, it wasn't a bad idea. And at least the horses would welcome his company.

Ross heard the commotion in stable four halfway between the house and the compound and took off at a run. He smelled smoke the second he tore open the doors. Fire! There was an orange glow at the end of the wide aisle of the building. He ran toward it and hit the alarm as he passed. It was set to ring in every building on the place and at the local fire station simultaneously. Help would arrive quickly. There was no greater enemy to a stable than fire. For some reason the sprinkler system hadn't come on, but he didn't have time to figure out what was wrong.

The door to the practice ring was aflame, and the fire was creeping up the wall. It was far beyond his ability to deal with on his own.

He cursed. This was his only stable without access to the yard from each stall. He'd have to turn the horses out into the yard using the central access doors rather than the ring. Since the fire was in front of the ring exit, that meant dragging almost a dozen horses toward the fire, unless he wanted to take a chance on them straying to the main road. In the confusion of a fire that could too easily happen.

Ross grabbed a blanket and opened the stall closest to the fire. Paddy's Pony, a big bay Irish Draught Thoroughbred mix, stood seventeen hands. Paddy's eyes rolled back, fear clearly overriding all his excellent training. The panicked gelding reared and caught Ross on the top of the shoulder with a sharp hoof, knocking him into the wall. He recovered quickly and managed to toss the blanket over the gelding's eyes. Typically, the animal quieted and Ross tucked the blanket around the halter and led him to safety.

Then Meg, Georgie and Manuel were there to help free the frightened animals. Ross went after Mischief, Cole's horse, but one of the others must have taken him out already. He went next after his own horses. He'd just turned toward Ross's Prize when he saw Amelia pulling Cobby, the old pony she'd taken such a shine to, toward safety. He hadn't thought his heart could pound any harder. Unused to horses—panicked ones, at that—she was having trouble with even this little guy. She hadn't covered his eyes, and he just wanted to hide in his stall.

Ross went to help Amelia, but Meg was in danger, struggling with a frightened stallion whose blanket had slipped off after she'd pulled him into the smoke-filled aisle. Ross tossed a blanket at Amelia with quick instructions to cover Cobby's eyes, then helped his sister calm the stallion and took him to the yard himself.

When he got back to check on her, Amelia wasn't there. He ran into the stable, where the smoke was growing thicker by the second. He shouted for her over the sounds of the screaming horses and the roar of the fire. A whooshing sound near the site of the fire drew him in that direction. He found Amelia fighting the fire with an extinguisher. She had a second one lying at her feet, as well. Ross wondered why she'd grabbed them instead of one of the high-pressure hoses but picked up the second extinguisher when he saw that she'd made headway against the flames. They worked side by side for several minutes, but fire still advanced up the wall and was licking at the rafters, raining tongues of flame all around them. When an ember dropped on Amelia's sleeve, Ross quickly extinguished it. He couldn't let her endanger herself for a building any longer.

"Come on," he shouted over the din of the fire, the horses and her extinguisher. "The horses are almost all out."

"Then you help Meg and Georgie get the rest. I'll try to keep this from spreading farther." She choked on the smoke.

Ross grabbed the extinguisher from her and tossed it to the side where he'd thrown his. "No. Let's go. Now."

Amelia looked as if she would protest, but Ross didn't give her time to balk. Pulling her against his side and wrapping his arm around her shoulder, he drew her toward the door. He told himself he only held her clutched at his side because she was a guest and his responsibility. He had himself half convinced it was true and that it had nothing to do with the fear he'd felt when he hadn't found her safe in the yard.

The building was being cleared by Meg, Georgie and Manuel, the handlers who lived at Laurel Glen. Amelia promised not to go back inside. Ross went to find out where Donovan was with the high-pressure hose. As he rounded the corner of the stable, Ross saw the foreman pound on the faucet with a wrench. From the look on Donovan's face, Ross knew there was more trouble.

"What's wrong with the water?" Ross demanded.

"We're not getting a trickle at this end! I thought maybe the valve was busted. It's not! The water's just not there!" Donovan shouted, his frustration evident.

Arson. The thought popped into Ross's head before he could stop it. And once it was there, he couldn't shake the dread that flooded him. A water pressure problem at the exact moment a fire erupted was an awfully big coincidence. Add the fire having occurred in the building where evacuation was most complicated, and arson was the only conclusion he could reach. Someone had tried to burn him out!

"Trace the water line," he ordered, turning to

Manuel, who ran up to them. "See what you can do to fix it. I want that water flowing ten minutes ago."

"Will do, boss," Manuel acknowledged.

"Come on, Donovan. Let's get the rest of the horses out." Ross saw Amelia and Meg putting the last section in a shoot fashioned out of pieces of the fence sections used for jump practice. The shoot linked the yard to the gate of the nearest pasture. His heart turned over seeing how determined Amelia was to help. He turned to follow Donovan into the building and saw Cole's Blazer roar up the drive.

His graceful son tripped and fell in his haste to get to the stable doors. Scrambling to his feet, Cole shouted something at Ross and ran inside the building by the doors Ross had entered when he'd found the fire. They met at the yard door minutes later, each with a horse in hand, and steered the animals into the improvised shoot.

"What did you say?" he asked Cole.

"Your phones are down. I called the fire department with my cell phone from the head of the drive when I saw the smoke. I didn't know what was on fire, but I knew something was. This had to be set!"

Without another word, Cole whirled and ran inside. Ross followed, stunned. He'd never have considered that the fire department might not be on the way. Without Cole's intervention they would have lost the whole building for sure. Now at least there was a chance, Ross thought as he dropped to one knee to take a deep breath of less smoky air before entering the next stall.

After several more trips, he met Cole frantically running from stall to stall. Georgie shouted an all clear, meaning all animals had been removed and that he was going to save some of the tack. But Cole continued his stall-by-stall check.

Ross grabbed his son by the shirt. "Come on. Georgie already checked," he shouted, coughing almost constantly now.

"Mischief," Cole yelled and shook him off. He, too, coughed violently as he headed deeper into the building where the fire was worst.

Ross, light-headed and out of breath, followed. He'd assumed one of the others had moved the horse, but now that he thought about it he hadn't seen Cole's distinctive gelding in the pasture with the rescued horses.

"I can't find him," Cole called, then stumbled over something and fell forward.

Ross gripped Cole's shoulders to keep him from falling, then he latched on to his son's arm. Cole yelped as if in pain, trying to pull away. Ross held on. "We're empty in here. Come on. Maybe they took him out the far door."

They staggered together into the yard and were greeted by the sound of sirens. "Fire department," Cole gasped and bent over, bracing his hands on his knees.

Ross greedily dragged in several lungs full of air

before answering. "A lot of good they'll do. Whoever did this got to the water." He blinked the soot from his burning eyes and started to help his son find the horse he'd risked his life to save. "Son, he's just not in there," Ross said, standing next to the fence, looking down the hill toward the milling horses.

When Cole didn't answer, Ross turned and found Cole, bent over in the middle of the yard still in the same position, a pain-filled expression on his face. "Cole?"

The expression in Cole's eyes when he pushed himself straight was one of bewilderment and helplessness. Ross had not seen that particular expression on his son's face since childhood. "We'll find Mischief. He's probably wandering down the drive," he told his son. Mischief was important to Cole. He'd rescued the animal from an abusive owner weeks after returning from California.

Cole nodded and took a deep breath, but his eyes still showed deep confusion. "How could someone hate this much?" he asked.

It was a question for which Ross had no answer, and he felt a deep kinship with his son for the first time in years.

Chapter Six

By the time the firemen spilled off their trucks, Manuel had returned with news that he'd found the place where someone had disrupted the water supply and he'd temporarily repaired the damage. The fire was quickly subdued. Considering the head start it had on the firefighters, Ross could only credit Amelia's attempt at firefighting for slowing it down.

All the excitement had begun to wind down, but the scene was still chaotic. Ross had to deal with firefighters, fire investigators and several owners who showed up worried for their animals.

It was going on eight-thirty, and darkness was falling when Ross got free. He went looking for Amelia to thank her for her help. She knocked him off balance emotionally, he admitted as he searched. His terror for her safety had been over and above what he should have felt for his sister's guest.

He conceded that now. He had to before he could deal with it.

And he had to deal with it. He would never give that kind of control to another person again. Marley had taught him well. So he'd thank Amelia and keep her at an emotional and physical distance from then on.

But all those plans flew out the proverbial window when Georgie pointed her out. She was standing at the back of an ambulance he hadn't noticed. Terror struck at his heart. For her. For himself. He relaxed when he realized she was only standing there talking to someone, but he soon grew concerned for another reason.

From fifty yards away, Ross could see she was livid. "Detective Lovell, you are not going to bother him right now!" he heard her declare.

Ross broke into a jog, reacting to the outrage in Amelia's voice. "What's going on?" he demanded when he got closer.

They both turned to face him, and for the first time Ross noticed someone sitting on the tailgate of the ambulance being treated by a paramedic. "Who's hurt?" he asked as Lovell walked forward to meet him.

"I don't want you two comparing notes before I question him," Lovell said, stepping in Ross's path and putting out a restraining hand. Ross sidestepped, but the detective latched on to his shoulder. A lot of factors went into what happened next. It was the same shoulder Paddy's Pony had stomped, and the moment the pain registered Ross realized Cole was the one being treated. Lovell found himself flat on his back staring at the darkening sky.

"What's wrong?" Ross demanded, close enough to see that Cole wore an oxygen mask. His son's eyes were closed, and his head rested on some sort of cabinet just inside the vehicle. Ross thought at first Cole might have inhaled too much smoke but just as quickly he realized the paramedic was bandaging Cole's arm.

"It's just a little burn," Cole muttered, and his voice, though a little shaky and muffled by the mask, was tight. It was a tone Ross had heard from his son all too often. Ross couldn't tell if it was pain or anger he heard, which gave him pause. Had he always misread Cole's emotions?

Amelia's heart went out to Ross. She could almost see the chains of the past that kept him from reaching out to his son. She glanced at Cole. His very stubborn son.

"He says one of those poles that make up the top sections of the stalls fell on him when he was looking for Mischief," Amelia told him before Cole could make light of the nasty burn she had only noticed by chance. "It must have burned free from the top support, and he put his arm up to stop it from hitting his head. Apparently it rolled along his arm on the way to the floor. He looked as if he was going into shock by the time I made him have it looked after. He also swears it doesn't hurt,'' Amelia said.

"It probably doesn't," the paramedic said. "He has a third-degree burn. Against my advice, he refuses to let us run him up to the hospital. Sir, he'll at least need to see someone as a follow-up. Considering his profession, he'll also need to be extremely careful of infection around animals."

"Could you stop talking about me as if I'm not here?" Cole muttered through the plastic oxygen mask.

Lovell stormed up. "I'll have you arrested for assaulting a police officer and obstructing an investigation, Taggert," he threatened Ross. The detective looked mad enough to spit nails.

Ross gave him a dead-eyed stare. "And I'll say you tripped. Even if I admit to giving you a shove, no judge in this county will do a thing to me when they hear you were keeping me from my injured son."

Lovell took a deep breath and seemed to take a mental step back. "You have to face the facts. You can't protect your son if he set that fire."

Ross narrowed his eyes. "You think Cole's behind this? Are you still playing that tune?"

Cole ripped off the oxygen mask and stood, however unsteadily. "I would never endanger a stable full of horses! Have you ever seen a horse trapped in a fire? Are you crazy, Lovell?"

"It was Cole who called the fire department," Ross told the detective. "We'd have lost the whole building without his intervention. Our phones are down so the automatic call didn't go through when I tripped the alarm. Cole wasn't even at Laurel Glen."

"Then how did you know the lines were down?" Lovell asked Cole.

"I called to talk to my aunt. I left, ah, abruptly and I wanted to square things with her about dinner. When no one answered at Laurel House, I got worried. There's always someone in the house to answer a phone, so I called an operator, and they said the phones weren't working. Considering all the incidents that have happened around here, I don't think that's too hard to understand. So I turned around and came back. When I got to the entrance, I saw smoke. Since the alarms notify the fire company through the phone lines, I called them in case no one here knew the phones were down."

"You say you left abruptly. Don't you mean you and your father had another argument? How do we know you didn't set the fire, then light out of here?"

"Do you really think I'd set a fire where I stable my own horse?"

"But your horse was in stable two, wasn't he?" Lovell charged. "He was as far from the fire as you could get him."

Cole looked confused. "I didn't know where he

was. The family's always used four. I left him in four. I was trying to find him when I—''

''I was in that burning stable with my son.'' Ross cut in, looking weary and on the edge. ''Cole was frantic and putting his life in danger trying to find that horse. He was burned because of how close he went to the fire looking for Mischief. Cole would never have taken a chance with his own life if he knew Mischief was safe elsewhere.''

''You have to admit my scenario makes sense,'' the detective countered.

''I don't have to admit anything. Cole didn't do this. I'm not going to tell you again. Look elsewhere for your suspect.''

''And I told you, I'll take this investigation wherever it leads, and no one is going to stop me.''

''Just make sure you look for the real person responsible. I don't want you taking the easy way out at the expense of this family.''

Lovell leveled a hard stare. ''I have never taken the easy road. I call them the way I see them, and your son looks as guilty as sin. If he is, I'll nail him. If he's being set up, I'll figure that out, too.'' Without another word he turned and stalked to his car.

Ross and Cole were both silent as they watched the detective get in his classic Mustang and drive off. ''He's right. I know it looks bad, but I didn't do this, Dad.''

Ross reared back and turned, dismay written on

his face. "I know you didn't. But what *was* Mischief doing in another stable?"

Amelia had a flash of insight, and it was too strong to ignore. "Cole wouldn't know because he didn't put him there. Someone is trying to destroy you, Ross. Or maybe it's just Laurel Glen they're after. And placing the blame on Cole is a good way to destroy confidence in the family as a whole. If they arrest your son, that's exactly what will happen. Whoever set the fire obviously moved Cole's horse to make Cole look guilty."

"But who'd be after me this way?" Ross asked. "And why? I don't have any enemies that I know of." He frowned, deep in thought. "I just don't."

"Didn't you say developers are buying up land around here? Is it possible that someone could be after your land?" Amelia asked.

"They wouldn't have to resort to driving me into bankruptcy. There's still plenty of land besides Laurel Glen available."

Cole shook his head. "But not prime land like this. We front two existing roads, and with Mom's land, we cover three linear miles on those roads. Maybe they know your reputation about the land and figured to do a little persuading first," Cole speculated. "Or have you gotten offers already?"

"I used to get feelers all the time, but I assume they got tired of my usual answer."

"What answer was that?" Amelia wondered.

Ross hesitated and glanced at the sky.

Cole snickered. "I think I mentioned the deterioration of your language, Dad."

Ross glared at Cole, but there was affection in his stern expression. "Suffice it to say, I said no in a way that no one would mistake it as a maybe."

"So it looks as if I'm one of the instruments of your destruction," Cole mused thoughtfully. "Maybe I should leave for a while. I still have to deal with the condo in California."

"Lovell said you couldn't leave town. I think he means it," Ross reminded him.

"Besides, if the theory that you're being framed is right, they'd stop doing this stuff while you're gone," Amelia added. "You'd look more guilty than ever when you came back if the incidents started again."

Cole sighed, obviously dispirited. "I think I'll go on up to the house and figure out how to take a shower and still keep my arm dry."

"There's a cast cover in my bathroom closet." Ross clapped his son on the shoulder and winced. "Try to get some rest."

Amelia watched Ross watching Cole walk toward the house. He carefully and slowly circled his shoulder and absently winced again. "He didn't do it. My son wouldn't hurt a fly."

Amelia nodded. "Of course he didn't. Maybe Detective Lovell will figure out who did, and this will all be over soon."

"Lovell's a fool."

"Not really. He found the most likely suspect in less than an hour that first afternoon he was on the case. Cole does look guilty. Remember, Detective Lovell doesn't know your son. He only knows what he sees, and the clues point to Cole. And you do look as if you're trying to cover for him."

"I'm not. I'm just being honest. Cole wouldn't do this."

"I'm sure he wouldn't. Just as I'm sure you're as stubborn as he is. Are you going to have this nice paramedic look at your shoulder?"

"Nah. There's nothing wrong with my shoulder. My dad's old fella just clipped me when I tried to move him."

"How much medical training did you say you've had?" she asked the paramedic who'd just hung up his cell phone.

The paramedic answered, and Amelia looked at Ross. "And how much medical training have you had, Mr. Taggert?"

Ross puffed air out in a long-suffering breath then sat on the tailgate in the light of the truck's rear spotlight. "I can move the shoulder fine. It's just a little stiff," he groused.

Grinning a little, the paramedic moved in and helped Ross out of his shirt. Amelia heard his breath hiss in the air. "Clavicle's busted," Ross said flatly. "Isn't it?"

"Looks like it, sir. If you don't want to go into

the ER then I'd suggest you get in touch with your orthopedic surgeon.''

''Yeah, yeah,' he said, clearly dismissing the excellent advice. ''It's not the first time. Probably won't be the last. Just give me a sling and I'll take care of it later.''

''But—''

Amelia saw the stubborn look on Ross's face that silenced the medic. Cole hadn't looked much different when she'd noticed the burn. She'd gotten him to the ambulance, but not until he'd checked over each and every horse rescued from stable four. The poor paramedic had certainly been put to the test that evening.

''I think that's as much of a concession as you'll get out of a Taggert. I'll tell his sister. She'll see that he does the right thing.''

''You'd set a man's own sister on him?'' Ross demanded.

''To stop the man from hurting himself? You bet I would.''

Ross sighed. ''You're a menace. I'll call the doctor in the morning.''

As they started for the house, headlights swept across them. It was the last piece of fire equipment pulling onto the drive leading to the main road. Ross had wiped most of the soot from his face, as she had, but otherwise they were pretty filthy. Amelia laughed. ''We need showers and something to eat. Neither of us had dinner.''

"I'm sorry," Ross said.

"Because I missed dinner? You didn't start the fire, either, Ross."

He shook his head and took her elbow, steering her toward Laurel House again. "I mean I'm sorry for snapping at you in the front parlor before all this started. I had no right to ask you a question then get mad when I didn't like the answer."

Amelia pondered a response until they'd nearly reached the house. She turned to him at the foot of the steps. "I was wrong, too. I spoke in anger because you act as if life on the other side of the Laurel Glen entrance is a perfect paradise. The road has had a few rocky times for the rest of us, too. Believe me. You were wrong, but I still should have spoken from the love of the Lord."

"I'm not convinced there is any." Ross stared at her, his blue eyes solemn. "Not for me, anyway. I'll see you later," he said stiffly but, oddly, he touched her cheek—a gentle, feather-light caress. And then he was gone. It felt as if he'd just said goodbye.

Chapter Seven

❧

Amelia finished her tea and set the glass aside then got back to the task of the moment—organizing her work. She leafed through scans of the photos she had yet to match and set aside those whose location she needed Ross's help to find.

After she had all the scans organized, she sat back to consider her options. Cole had helped her quite a bit at the historical society in the week since the fire. He'd had a lot of free time because the risk of infection was too great for him to work around horses with the severe burn he'd suffered in the stable fire. Unfortunately, because of his generous help, she had nothing left to do before writing the text of the book except the interviews, and shots she needed Ross's help to get.

Her shutter finger itched to move ahead with the photo shoots, but she saw little chance of that. The broken collarbone was supposed to have freed up a lot of Ross's time, as well, but though he'd been promising for a week to take her to get shots, he'd disappeared before breakfast was over. She hadn't seen him since. According to Meg, who had left an hour earlier for a luncheon meeting at the historical society, he was avoiding her. She would have asked Cole if he could help but he'd gone to a meeting with the old veterinarian who was selling his practice.

Amelia and Cole had spent a good deal of time together in the past week, especially since his father was among the missing most of the time. It had worked out well, though. The night of the fire she'd decided to befriend the younger man, hoping to help him deal with his anger toward Ross. They'd become friendly, but Cole wouldn't let her get too close. Amelia thought that perhaps he didn't let anyone get past the amiable teasing face he turned to the world. And he absolutely wouldn't talk about his mother or the accident that killed her. It was as if there was something he couldn't face about her death, and talking about it brought him closer to the truth of it.

Too close.

Amelia pushed Cole's problems from her mind. She was getting too involved in the problems between father and son. It tied her stomach in knots whenever she thought about it. She wanted to help but she wasn't the one who needed to fix the problem. It was up to Ross and Cole. Feeling her patients' pain too deeply was the reason she'd nearly had a breakdown during her internship just short of getting her degree in psychology.

She'd trained for a profession where someone with her personality didn't belong. Subconsciously she'd been trying to be what her mother wanted her to be. It had taken her father to make her see that she'd subverted her dreams, trying to make up for a past that would remain unchanged no matter what she did in the present.

Amelia wandered to the window, determined to put the past and at least the troubling part of the present out of her thoughts. She sighed then took a deep breath. Calmer, she took in the sun-drenched sky with its big fluffy clouds scudding above the horizon. Today the temperature was in the low eighties with little appreciable humidity, which was a treat in the Delaware Valley's dog days of summer.

And it was a perfect day to take those pictures! But with both Cole and Meg occupied, she was stuck in the house and completely at loose ends. If there was one thing Amelia Howard couldn't stand, it was being bored or wasting time. Today looked as if it she might wind up doing both!

Determined, she set off to find Ross. He was the one who'd made her promise not to go anywhere unaccompanied, so the logjam in the flow of her work was about to become his problem to solve. He wasn't in the house. Against his decree, she went looking for him outside.

When Amelia found Ross at the practice ring all her annoyance melted. He stood at the fence with a small girl balanced in front of him, her little booted feet on the rails, her pudgy arms looped over the top of the fence. They were watching an older child take her horse through a series of exercises in the ring. Man and toddler were chatting like old friends.

"…in a year or two. Would you like that?" Ross was saying to the tiny girl when Amelia got close enough to hear.

The towheaded child nodded, her curls bobbing, but then she turned her head and looked at Ross, her bottom lip pouting. "I wanna ride horsie now," she cried.

Ross kissed her on the top of her golden head. "Hey, Robert," he yelled to one of the handlers. "Toss a saddle on Cobby. Let's see Emily here do her stuff."

The child's eyes widened. "Oh, can I?"

"You're sure this isn't too much trouble or that she isn't too young?" the woman next to them asked. Amelia assumed she was the children's mother.

"Nah. Cole started riding Cobby when he was younger than this young lady here. And believe it or not, Hope was on the old boy practically before she could walk." He bent and whispered something to the woman that made her laugh.

Amelia backed off and watched Ross give the three-year-old girl her first riding lesson. It was magical for everyone. Camera in hand, Amelia recorded the event with a telephoto so as not to intrude. When the children were done and loaded in their mother's car, Amelia approached Ross and the woman.

"Hi. The little one seems to be a natural," she said.

The young mother laughed. "She's been practicing on a hobby horse for a year now. We hear that infernal squeak in our sleep. I wish my husband could have been here."

"Well, I know it's not the same, but I shot a couple rolls of film. They should be back from my lab in a week or so."

The woman's eyes widened. "You're Amelia Howard. Oh, goodness, you really are. I recognize you from the picture on the cover jacket of *America the Beautiful*. It's my favorite!"

Embarrassed, Amelia smiled. She'd never get used to people recognizing her. "Guilty as charged. I'll give the prints to Ross, and he can pass them on to you."

"Oh, I love your work. No one's going to believe this. *I* don't believe this. Amelia Howard took pictures of Emily's first lesson. Thanks so much. I can't wait to tell Alan."

When mother and children had bumped out of the yard and were on their way down the drive, Ross turned and crossed his arms. "I thought I wasn't supposed to recognize your name. She recognized your face.''

Amelia shrugged. ''I guess she has one of my books. That was really sweet of you giving the little one that impromptu lesson.''

Embarrassed, Ross frowned. ''It was business. Now they'll start lessons on Cobby for little Emily.''

''Oh. I forgot. The tough-guy image. We're supposed to preserve it. Hmm.'' Amelia waved the film canisters in the air. ''These would be real blackmail material, then. Especially the one of you planting a kiss on Emily's sweet little blond head.'' Amelia smiled broadly. ''You, sir, are a fraud. *And* an old softy.''

Amelia dropped the film in her bag, determined to find out why he'd been avoiding her. ''So if you're such a sweetheart, how come you keep breaking your promises to me? You can't ride. Georgie had to help with the older child's lesson because you can't raise your arm. So how come you can't take me out to do the interviews and to take the shots I need?''

''I thought you and Cole were spending most of your time together these days. I didn't think my help was required.''

Was she imagining the slight edge of annoyance in his voice? Had he mistaken her and Cole's growing friendship for something more? Something romantic? She wasn't sure if that was a good thing or not. He could be jealous of her time with Cole, which would be good if he'd wanted that time with her, or he might think a romance between her and his son was inappropriate because of their age difference.

"Oh? Why would you think I didn't want your help? Meg asked you to show me where the old homesteads were, and you promised you would. But after the fire you suddenly had so much to do that we've scarcely seen you. I've been spending time with Cole because his doctor restricted him from any contact with the horses. He was at loose ends, and I was grateful for his research help. Your son's a nice person. Is there a problem with my being his friend?"

Ross stiffened and held the fence in a death grip. "No. No, of course not."

"Good, because he needs a friend right now."

"I love my son, all evidence to the contrary. I want good things for him. He deserves some happiness. If you make him happy, then I'm happy."

Amelia frowned. He *did* believe she and Cole were becoming romantically involved! "I don't think you understand, Ross. I said *friend*," she told him patiently. "As in someone to talk to. I think there's something deeper bothering Cole than his mother's death and the way she died. I hoped if he felt comfortable with me, I could get him to talk. He hasn't as yet, but friendship is all that's between us."

Ross nodded, his brow knitted. "It turns out that

I'm free for the rest of the day. Do you want to see how many of those places on your list we can hit?''

The day instantly seemed brighter. Amelia beamed him a wide smile. "That's what I was hoping you'd say. I have to pick up more film at the house first, though. I didn't plan on the pony lessons.''

Ross started his 4×4 and pulled it around in front of the house. He didn't know what had gotten into him. Why had he admitted he didn't have anything planned for the rest of the day? He'd plead temporary insanity, but he was very afraid that if he had to do it while looking into Amelia's gray-sky eyes he'd wind up offering her the world. He didn't seem to be able to deny her anything. That was why he kept promising to escort her on her day trips in the mornings and coming to his senses later, once he got away from her.

He tooted the horn then caught his reflection in the side mirror. He was being really stupid about her. He might be attracted to her, but if she saw a good-looking young stud like Cole as a friend, she probably saw Ross as a father figure. Though it would be safer, he did not want to be a father figure to Amelia Howard.

Feeling a little insulted, he leaned on the horn again. There might be eleven years between them, and he might be too old for her, but he was *not* old enough to be her father!

"I'm coming. I'm coming," Amelia yelled as she scrambled down the steps. "What's your hurry?"

Ross smacked the steering wheel. Now she had him acting like an impatient teenager honking for his date! Ross shrugged to cover his chagrin when she climbed in next to him. "Hey, you're the one losing the light," he said carelessly. He hoped! "Take your time. I just wanted you to know I wasn't holding up the train. Where to first?"

"Diamond Rock School House. Meg says it's eighteenth-century octagon architecture. I thought since some of the people I'm writing about went to school there, it might make a nice cover for the book."

"Old Diamond Rock School it is, then. Fasten your seat belt, Ms. Howard. The train's pullin' out!"

Ross watched Amelia all day. She didn't just take pictures. She treated each shot as if the world was her canvas and the camera her paint. He'd always thought photographers walked around clicking hundreds of shots, had them developed then kept the best. Amelia worked with light and changed filters and lenses the way an artist would brushes. She was serious and dedicated and an absolute perfectionist. He couldn't wait to see the finished product. And he intended to look for the books Meg had of her previous work.

It was seven-fifteen, and she was still at it, using the setting sun as a backdrop for the decaying barn on what was left of the Abernathy homestead. The property was up for sale, the house boarded up, waiting for some developer to take on its marshy land and limited access to even a minor road.

"I guess that about wraps it up for today," he called a few minutes later when he saw that she'd begun packing up her camera bag.

Amelia walked over and hopped on the tailgate to sit next to him. "When it's raining, I dream of days like this one. What a sunset!"

Ross followed her gaze to the blue and pink sky. The red-golden sun had almost dropped behind the trees. Then his eyes trailed to a truly incredible sight.

Amelia.

Her eyes were alive with happiness, her smiling bottom lip caught just slightly under her top teeth. Of its own volition his heart started pounding and his breathing quickened, deepened. He didn't want her to move away from him but to move into his aching arms.

"My mother called that sky-blue-pink. Incredible," she said reverently.

Ross couldn't seem to get his eyes to look at anything but her. "Yeah. Incredible," he agreed, staring at Amelia's peaches-and-cream skin. He'd touched that skin the night of the fire, swearing as he did that it meant goodbye. He'd thought it was. But she was every temptation he'd ever faced all rolled into one lovely package. And so far he hadn't found a defense.

He had the edge of the tailgate in a death grip to keep himself from repeating his near fatal mistake. "We'd better get a move on," he said in the hope that driving would take his mind off his unruly needs. "That drive in was bad enough in full light. I don't want to be dodging those potholes in the dark."

Amelia laughed, and Ross's stomach did a quick flip. "Potholes? Where I come from, sir, those are called excavations. But whatever you call them, I guess you're right. It's just so peaceful here. You know?"

In danger of dragging her into his arms and kissing her senseless, Ross jumped off the tailgate but, as he turned to urge her to get a move on, she slid to the ground in front of him. The most natural and stupid thing he could have done was to lean down and cover her upturned mouth with his. And he did. Then he found himself sliding his hand into her hair and anchoring her to him, prolonging the kiss until he felt her hand on his chest gently urging him away.

Stupid, he thought. Didn't you decide she wasn't interested? Ross silently castigated himself and stepped back from her.

"I think we'd better go," she whispered, her voice soft as velvet and dark as midnight.

Ross nodded and went to climb into the cab. He

should have held the door for her but he couldn't risk getting that close again. He knew he should apologize but couldn't bring himself to pretend he wouldn't do it again given the same circumstances. She just plain blew all his intentions to smithereens.

"I'm, ah," he began, not knowing what to say but needing to break the silence.

"If you apologize, I'll post copies of that picture of you and Emily on every bulletin board in Chester County."

He smiled. He couldn't help that, either. She just made him happy. Maybe he wasn't too old for her, after all. "No apology. No explanation. Just an excuse. I haven't kissed a woman in fourteen years. You tempt me, Amelia Howard. And I don't know if that's a good thing or not. But with the research on this book of yours wrapping up, I don't see as I'll have time to figure it out. Maybe I'm a slow mover but—"

"I was going to ask your help on a second project. I don't want to outstay my welcome, but I've never been on a horse farm before. I find it fascinating. One thing I've learned since coming here is that love of horses has its roots in childhood. I've thought for a long time of branching into children's books, and I've been getting ideas for days about one on the inner workings of a place like Laurel Glen. It wouldn't be exactly a how-to on horse farming, but a story of a boy on an average day, week, month or even year who lives on a horse farm.

"I wouldn't need to stay that long, of course, but you could tell me about the long-term stuff and the different things that happen with the horses in each season. I also need to know the ways children can help out."

"You think there's a market for something like that?"

"There's a real cowboy mystique all over the world. Laurel Glen is in effect an eastern horse ranch, and you and your men are eastern cowboys. In fact that's a great title. *The Eastern Cowboy.* So what do you say?"

Chapter Eight

He'd said yes. He'd lost his mind and said yes.

It was six hours later, and Ross still couldn't believe he'd agreed to have Amelia stay at Laurel Glen for an indefinite period of time. And to make matters worse, she was going to be spending a large amount of that time with him learning about life on a horse farm.

He should have been asleep hours ago but instead he lay there in his bed, staring at the ceiling. Her presence in the house haunted him. Her presence and the look Cole had given him when the subject of Amelia's changed plans had come up at the dinner table. The look had been one that spoke of betrayal. So now he worried that Cole had begun to have feelings for Amelia. Did he think Ross was horning in on his territory? Or did his son see Ross's interest in Amelia as a final betrayal of Marley?

Betraying Marley. That was so funny it was almost laughable, but Ross had vowed long ago that neither of his children would ever know the truth about their mother. That truth haunted him enough for all of them.

Ross thought that maybe he'd let the secret he carried in his heart rule his life for too long. After all, *all* women weren't like Marley. Granny hadn't been. Meg and Hope certainly weren't. Neither, he was beginning believe, was Amelia.

Ross rolled out of bed, walked to the floor-to-ceiling windows in the sitting area of his room and looked over the paddocks and pastures. His domain. Master of all he surveyed.

What a crock!

He was barely keeping it together. It wasn't so much that he was personally in financial trouble because of the way Jeff, his new son-in-law, had advised him to split up his assets into personal and corporate divisions. But the business end of Laurel Glen was sinking fast.

The burned skeleton of stable four's roofline drew his eye. He hadn't been able to hide news of the fire from his clients. Not after the *Philadelphia Inquirer* hit the stands the next morning, anyway. It had been a slow news day, and a picture of stable four ablaze had made the front page of the Chester County section of the big Philly paper. "Arson at Local Horse Farm!" Ross muttered the headline that had burned itself into his brain.

He wasn't even sure he'd rebuild number four. There seemed little reason other than pride. He certainly didn't need the room. Several of the clients who'd remained loyal in the face of the rumors of carelessness had moved their stock, promising to return their animals as soon as the culprit was caught. It was a safety issue, they'd all assured him, not a lack of confidence in him. Even so, he wasn't about to hold his breath until their trailers rolled back under the Laurel Glen arch.

Ross scrubbed his hand over his face, knowing he had to get some sleep. As he turned to the bed, he let his hand trail down the finely carved woodwork of the window casement. You don't find work like this anymore, he thought, a wave of nostalgia swamping him. Laurel House would celebrate her one-hundred-and-fiftieth birthday next year. This land had been in his family for almost double that. He couldn't—wouldn't—be the one to lose even a part of what he'd built it into. If he had to use the assets Jeff had talked him into separating from the business part of Laurel Glen, he would. They—whoever *they* were—were not getting hold of his and his children's heritage by fair means or foul.

Amelia skidded to a halt inside the shadowed interior of the lower story of the big multilevel barn. The walls were ancient stone, and the floor, an obvious add-on, was smooth concrete, like the garage at the house where her currently worthless Jeep sat.

There were various vehicles and machines parked around the perimeter of the massive, eight-sided room.

Two tractors sat in varying stages of being dismantled or assembled. "Ross?" she called to the body beneath one of them.

The unmistakable sound of a head being bumped followed by a spate of less than sterling language followed. The body rolled out. It wasn't Ross but Laurel Glen's foreman, Harry Donovan. "Sorry, miss. For the language, I mean." He rubbed his head.

"Sorry I startled you. I was looking for Ross."

He grinned. "I kind of figured that, since it was his name you called."

Amelia chuckled when he scratched his nose then looked at his greasy hands in disgust.

"I thought you were the foreman—not the mechanic."

"I'm that, too. If something's broke around here, it's Harry Donovan and his toolbox to the rescue."

"Does my car qualify, do you think?" she asked. "It won't start, and I don't have a clue who to call. That's one of the reasons I was looking for Ross. To find out who to call," she added.

"Well, now. I'll just have to fit you in. Hope's got the same model as you, if I'm not mistaken, and I've always taken care of hers. I'd be insulted if you called in a mechanic. I've even taken a few courses in the electronics on those newer babies. Real fascinating stuff.''

Amelia smiled. She couldn't imagine describing grease and electronics as fascinating but she was grateful Harry Donovan felt that way. "Thanks so much, Mr. Donovan. I'll leave the keys in the ignition. Not that they'll do you much good, since it won't start."

"It's just plain Donovan. Harry was my father. I can't promise when, but I'll get to it. As for Ross, he was upstairs last I saw."

Amelia left in search of Ross. She walked up the embankment to the upper story of the barn. That put her on the driveway level. When she slid open the big barn door she looked around, surprised at the incongruous mix of functions this level fulfilled. There were barn things, like a hayloft and tools hanging neatly on the back wall. But there were also several offices that housed high-tech computers and modern desks, and men's and ladies' rooms.

Just inside the main door on both sides, forming a wide hallway, were Laurel Glen's offices and rest rooms. Each office was lined with old-fashioned varnished knotty pine. She found Ross in the last office. He was seated on a worn hunter-green leather sofa, reading a book.

"Hi, there," she said and knocked at the open doorway. "Donovan said you'd be here somewhere."

Ross looked up, his blue eyes peering over the

top of glasses she'd never seen him wear before. He looked vulnerable for the first time. A little less than bigger than life. He took off his glasses and dropped them next to him, then flipped the book shut. It was her last book. "You're very talented," he said, his tone almost grave.

Uncomfortable with praise and with his serious mood, she cast about for another subject. Her gaze fell on the glasses. "And you're nearsighted," she said, grinning, hoping to tease him into a lighter mood.

He stood. Sometimes his height was a surprise when he stood close to her. This was one of those times. She was tempted to retreat when he moved closer, but it was a small room, and she wasn't about to be backed into the hall.

"No, I'm not nearsighted at all," Ross said. "They're drugstore glasses. Do you know what that means?"

Unable to find her voice again, Amelia shrugged.

"It means I'm getting old—too old for you," he continued. "I nearly convince myself of that, but then you walk into a room and I don't feel old at all. I don't know what I do feel, other than the kinds of things I haven't felt for years. And old sure isn't one of them."

"Is that good or bad?"

Ross shook his head and stepped closer. His scent—soap, leather and some sort of limy spice—enveloped her and made her all jumpy and nervous-feeling, but she didn't think nervous was really the right word.

He was going to kiss her again. She swallowed hard and looked into his eyes. They didn't look old to her, and she told him so in a surprisingly husky whisper just before his lips settled on hers. He didn't feel old, either. His chest, when she settled her hand over his pounding heart, was hard and strong. The arm that pulled her close was strong, too. But the fingertips he trailed over her cheek were amazingly gentle.

No one's lips on hers had ever felt so right—so tender yet unyielding, so glorious yet terrifying. Terrifying for good reason, she thought when he began to deepen the kiss and any clarity of thought she'd had turned to mist and vapor. It made no sense that just his nearness and the pressure and caress of his lips could make her feel so loved and make her feel so much love for him in return.

But this couldn't be love to Ross. Ross loved another, and that the woman was dead made it all the more heartbreaking. Amelia didn't have a clue how to compete with the memory of a woman so dearly held that no one would even talk about her. She didn't even know if she wanted to try.

Before she was tempted to fool herself that this was more than a physical attraction to Ross, Amelia pressed her hand against his chest where it covered his thundering heart. But he didn't have the time to do more than ease the pressure of his lips and the arm banded around her when a gasp from behind made him push her away and whirl to face the intruder.

"Daddy?" a female voice questioned.

Amelia dropped her forehead against Ross's back. His broad shoulders blocked her view, and she was grateful. These were not the circumstances under which she'd meant to meet his daughter.

"Uh, Hope," Ross stammered. "What are you doing, uh, I mean, I didn't know you were, um—"

Hope chuckled. "We came home early because the trip tired Jeff more than he thought it would. And I'm standing in the doorway of my office because I promised to help you find my replacement as soon as I got back."

Amelia straightened and ran her fingers through her tangled hair, glad she wore her hair in carelessly ordered curls. She backed up a step as Hope, a teasing smile on her face, leaned to the right and gave Amelia a little wave.

"Aren't you going to introduce me to your friend, Daddy? At least I assume you're friends, considering," Hope said lightly.

"It's not what you think," Ross said.

Amelia stepped away from him, thankful she'd already remembered Marley but still surprised by the pain his disclaimer caused.

"Well, I certainly hope it is," Hope countered.

"But…your mother—"

Hope's raised eyebrow seemed to silence Ross.

"My mother is dead and has been for a good many years. It's time to start living again, Daddy. For all of us. Now why don't you apologize to the nice lady while I go visit with Aunt Meg. We'll meet later, Amelia. And by the way, I like your books, but I like most of all the effect you seem to have on my foot-in-the-mouth father. Keep up the good work." She waved and was gone, leaving a heavy silence in her wake in spite of her efforts to lighten things a bit.

Ross reached for Amelia, but she took another step back. "Don't," she ordered, wishing her voice sounded stronger.

"I'm sorry," he said, clearly at a loss for a defense.

"For what, Ross? The kiss? Or that it meant nothing to you?"

His eyes burned like twin flames. "It mustn't have meant all that much to you, either. You were pushing me away just the way you did last night."

Amelia wondered if she should be honest or try to salvage her pride. Honesty won, as it usually did with her. "I didn't push you away because it meant nothing, Ross. I pushed you away because it meant too much. Apparently it's a good thing I did, since it meant a whole lot more to me than it did to you."

She shouldered her way past him, ignoring his stunned expression and the hand that brushed her shoulder as she passed. She kept walking, unfit for company at the moment.

Amelia was furious, hurt, confused and determined. Furious because she hadn't listened to Meg and her own good sense about the possibility of a future with Ross. Hurt that he could use her so carelessly and be so like the men she'd thought him a cut above. Confused because even though it was clear he wasn't able to give even a portion of his heart to someone other than Marley, she still cared for him—deeply.

And finally determined. Determined to return to Laurel House and pack! She couldn't stay. Because she did still care, and Ross's indifference would hurt too much to let her endure his company.

Amelia turned to do just that and looked around, expecting to see Laurel House high on the hill behind her. But all she could see was underbrush and scrub trees stunted by the dense growth of towering pines and deciduous trees. After turning in every direction to look for the house that overlooked everything in the vicinity, she could no longer remember which direction she'd come from. One tree looked like another in dense woodlands, and she hadn't been paying attention to anything but her inner thoughts. Nor could she remember starting on what was probably only a deer trail that had dozens of others crisscrossing it.

She dropped down on a nearby rock. This was why she never went anywhere without a guide. Once lost in thought or taking shots of nature, everything else flew from her head. But that was neither here nor there. She was lost and thirsty, and it was getting really hot and muggy even in the darkness of the shadowed woods.

And no one at the farm knew she was missing, either.

She smacked at a bug that landed on her arm. About the only thing she had going for her was that she'd gotten a Lyme disease vaccination in the spring as a precaution. And it was a good thing, since the disease had moved into Pennsylvania with a vengeance, and she was smack in the middle of deer territory.

Looking around at the predicament she was in, Amelia shook her head in disgust and pushed herself to her feet. No one was going to rescue her from her foolhardy venture, and truth be told, she didn't want rescuing. She'd told Ross he'd have no reason to baby-sit her while she was a guest at Laurel Glen, and she didn't want to give him one. Besides, she never wanted to see or talk to him again if she could avoid it.

An hour later, she sat with her foot soaking in a minuscule stream, rethinking her bold declaration. At that point she'd probably kiss Ross's feet if she saw him. She might even kiss a familiar road if she came upon one, for that matter, so Ross Taggert shouldn't feel honored, she added grimly. She'd tried to keep the sun at her back, thinking that if she walked in the same direction for any length of time she'd be sure to stumble on some vestige of civilization. So far the only thing she'd stumbled on was a hole that had probably been some little animal's home. It had been her Waterloo! Her ankle was definitely sprained, and things were looking a little grim.

At lunchtime, Ross headed for the house though he still didn't know what to say to Amelia. He hadn't meant to act as if the kiss meant nothing to him. It *had* meant something. He had been flummoxed by Hope's appearance, and besides, he really wasn't sure what the kiss had meant. Just that it had meant *something*. They were friends, but the kiss had gone beyond friendly. Way beyond his definition of friendship, anyway. No, it hadn't been a friendly kiss.

He'd felt as if he'd suddenly awakened to find the perfect woman in his arms, but he couldn't say that. It would sound too much like some kind of commitment. He was nowhere near ready to admit anything like that, especially since the kiss had evidently meant so much to Amelia. He didn't know what to say to her, but he had to think of something.

"Well, you're looking grim," Meg quipped when he entered the breakfast room where the family gathered for the first two meals of the day.

Hope looked up from a notebook she had at her place. "Did you make it up to Amelia?"

"She wouldn't listen."

"Daddy, I hope you had the sense to follow her and make her listen."

Ross shrugged. "I really didn't have anything to say. I thought I'd let her cool off for a while. Where is she, anyway?"

Meg and Hope looked at each other.

"Well?" he urged when they looked at him blankly.

"Ross, we thought…we *hoped* you two were in the barn making up. Neither of us have seen her. Maybe she's in her room. And maybe you should go apologize again," Meg suggested.

"But I still don't—"

"Now!" his sister ordered. "Discounting the kind of kiss Hope says she interrupted with a woman like Amelia is about as unforgivable as it gets. Still, you'll never regret anything more if you don't try."

Muttering about bossy women, Ross went up the back stairs to find Amelia. But she wasn't in her room. Ten minutes later he admitted that she wasn't in the house at all. Her car was parked where she'd left it, but none of the house staff had seen her. He didn't like her wandering around by herself with a potential killer roaming the farm. Meg and Hope were worried about that, too.

The phone rang just as he started to walk out the back door on his way to check the barn. Hope answered it and waved him in.

"You were what? Jeffrey Carrington, you are *not* allowed to ride yet! How could—" Hope stopped her diatribe. "You did? Okay, hold on a minute. I'll check." She spoke to Ross. "A while ago I called Jeff and told him about all the trouble you've been having while we were gone, and he just remembered something. He was out riding a couple hours ago and saw a woman walking south toward Laurel Glen's border. He thought we should know. Aunt Meg, when I saw Amelia in the barn, I didn't get a very good look at what she was wearing. Do you know?"

"White sneakers and ankle socks. Navy shorts and a pale-blue sleeveless shirt with little tiny white flowers on it," Ross reported, remembering every detail of the woman who had captivated him with her fresh-as-springtime image.

Hope stared at him in amazement. "You remember what she was *wearing?* Oh, I really have to get to know this woman."

"What's so odd about me knowing what she was wearing? I'm observant!" Ross maintained, and wondered why Hope rolled her eyes at his claim.

"Did you get that?" Hope asked her new husband. "It fits the woman you saw? Good. I love you, too."

"I have to get out there looking for her," Ross said. "She could be lost or hurt. Or in danger."

Hope nodded. "I'll ride out with you."

"Count me in, too," Meg said. "We'll cover three times the territory that way."

Ross nodded, picked up the phone and ordered

their three horses saddled with Western saddles. In less than five minutes he was headed south with Meg and Hope not far behind. He rode hard, worry and some unnamed terror driving him. He never even noticed when Meg and Hope peeled off in the opposite direction. Ross refused to think it was fear that it might be too late to salvage a relationship with her when he wasn't even sure he could handle one.

Chapter Nine

Amelia braced herself on the branch she'd been using as a makeshift crutch and took another painful step. This one took her out of the trees and to the edge of a clearing. "Yes!" she shouted, seeing she was nearly at the top of a hill that was blessedly free of anything green but tall grass and the odd wildflower.

With nothing in her path to trip her, it took only a few minutes to reach the crest. However, any feeling of triumph fled when she saw nothing familiar. There was a flat rock partially shaded by the tree line, so she limped over to it. The rock was at the crest of a hill overlooking a small valley. She sank gratefully to its smooth, warm surface.

As she'd limped through the dense woods, Amelia had speculated on two things. One—that she was moving steadily uphill and had been for the last half hour of her interminable trek through southeastern Pennsylvania's woodlands. Two—she was utterly lost with a capital L.

Being right, she found, was a small comfort.

Glancing at the strong sun, Amelia sighed in disgust. She'd be burned to a crisp if she strayed out of the shade for very long. Which left her three possibilities. Fight the underbrush again, which had already scratched her arms and legs, risk a sunburn by charging ever forward or sit on the shaded end of the rock and wait for rescue like a wilting damsel in distress.

She hated the wilting damsel scenario, but when she looked at her swollen ankle, she had to admit it was the most practical option. Amelia blew out a breath and looked longingly downhill. She blinked and straightened, squinting against the harsh sunlight.

Is that a horse and rider coming toward me, or am I hallucinating?

Amelia stood and waved the branch. "Hey! Up here," she shouted, and was rewarded when the rider pulled his mount to a halt and looked around. "Here!" she yelled and waved again, just resisting the urge to jump up and down with glee when the rider looked right at her. It was Ross.

Amelia's heart began to pound. What was she going to say to him? And why did he have to come looking for her on horseback? Wasn't it bad enough that she was nervous about seeing him so soon after their tiff without the added worry of riding home atop one of his oversized beasts?

She straightened her shoulders and spine, determined not to let him see how nervous he and his mode of transportation made her.

She took a deep breath, planning to apologize for troubling him. But before she got the chance to say she was sorry, he was practically flying out of the saddle and pulling her into his arms. He kissed her quickly then wrapped her in his strong embrace.

"I've been so worried since I realized you were gone. I'm so sorry," he said, then let her loose, holding her at arm's length. "Look at you. You're all scratched up. You don't go hiking dressed like this, woman!"

"This wasn't exactly a planned hike," Amelia admitted, her head spinning from his kiss and her conscience tweaked by his worry. She should have been more understanding. If Meg was right, Ross hadn't dated since his teen dates with Marley. Hope's sudden appearance in the office would have rattled him. "I'm sorry. It was a temper tantrum—pure and simple. I was wrong to storm off that way, Ross. It was childish. I never meant to be gone so—"

Ross gently covered her lips with his finger. "Hush. You had every right. I was a jerk. A fool. It's just that Hope isn't used to seeing me kiss women. She's not used to even seeing me with a woman. Heck, I'm not used to it. Before I knew what I was saying, I was sticking my size twelve in my big mouth."

"I realize this is new to you. Now, anyway. I shouldn't have stomped off that way. I'm sorry."

"I just didn't have a clue what to say to Hope. If she was going to blow a gasket, I didn't want you exposed to it. Especially after the way Cole reacted at dinner last night."

"He did seem a little surprised that I'd spoken to you about staying before I did Meg," Amelia admitted, forgetting her ankle. The second she put her full weight on it she yelped and plunged unceremoniously to the ground before Ross could catch her.

"What is it?" Ross asked, on his knees beside her at once.

Amelia felt her face heat. "I forgot to mention that I sprained my ankle and hour or so ago."

Ross looked puzzled. "An hour or more? Then you continued walking away from Laurel Glen after you got hurt? Were you that mad at me?"

Amelia shot him a wry grin. "Did I also forget to mention that I was kind of...sort of..." She huffed out a quick disgusted breath. "I was hopelessly lost out here, Ross."

He sat on his heels, tipped his hat back and grinned. His blue eyes sparkled. "Well, yeah. You kind of—sort of—did forget to mention that. Is this the reason you always hire a guide?"

Amelia refused to answer on principle. "I was distracted."

"Distracted? Do you have any idea how long you were gone? Or how far you walked? We've got to be almost six miles southwest of Laurel House."

"Very distracted, then!"

Ross laughed. "I'll call the others and tell them I've got you, then let's get a look at that ankle."

"Others?" she asked, cringing at the idea of having caused such a stir.

"Meg and Hope only. Cole was gone, so he isn't out looking. I was leery of letting anyone outside the family know you were alone out here. I don't know who to trust or how far whoever is causing all the trouble will go to destroy Laurel Glen."

Ross took out his cell phone and let his sister and daughter know Amelia was safe, then helped her onto the warm flat rock. Amelia sucked in air sharply when he pulled her shoe off.

Ross winced. "Sorry. I don't think it's broken, but sprains can be just as painful. I've got a first aid kit with me. I'll wrap it then get you back to Laurel House. How's that sound?"

She smiled at him. "Is there a glass of sweet tea waiting for me?"

"A gallon of it, if that's what you want," he promised, his deep blue eyes sparkling in the sunlight.

Amelia marveled at the ability of so strong a man to be so very gentle as she watched him wrap her ankle. On his knees at her feet Ross bent his dark head to his task. He seemed completely unaware of how deeply his gentle care touched her. Finally she closed her eyes, letting his careful ministrations soothe her bruised heart as well as her injury. He wouldn't take such sweet care of her if she meant nothing to him, she assured herself.

Then he was by her side, urging her to lean into him and allow him to support her head on his strong shoulder. "I never meant to hurt you."

"I feel silly about being hurt. I guess feeling as I do about you has made me vulnerable."

He went still. "Uh, yeah. It is pretty new. I think we'd better get you back."

Amelia hobbled to the counter by the light of the open refrigerator, trying to negotiate with her crutches and the nearly full gallon bottle of milk. She'd just set down the bottle and reached for a glass when the door from the garage burst inward. She yelped and dropped the plastic glass she'd wisely chosen. It bounced across the tile floor, then she lost her hold on the unwieldy crutches and sent them crashing to the floor. They landed at Cole's feet next to the glass.

"Oh, goodness, you scared me," she said when she saw who it was.

Cole bent and picked up the things she'd dropped. The crutches he leaned against the counter, and he put the glass in front of her. "The door was stuck," he said, explaining his forceful entry. "What on earth are you doing? Are you trying to wreck that ankle for good? Suppose you put too much weight on it. A sprain is nothing to fool with."

"Yes, doctor," Amelia quipped.

"Good attitude. I'm used to cooperative patients. Now get over on that banquette and sit. I'll get your milk."

Amelia shrugged and moved to the padded bench at the little kitchen table. The grouping was a small cozy oasis in the corner of the efficient kitchen. The first time she'd seen it she'd thought it was perfect for midnight raids on the fridge or soothing cups of tea before dawn.

Cole followed and lit a candle in the middle of the table, then closed the refrigerator door. "I'll be right back," he said, and disappeared only to return with a pillow for under her foot and one for behind her back where she leaned against the wall. The up-holstered bench was at once a comfy chaise.

"Okeydoke," Cole said and shot her a grin. "Now that you're comfortable, what were you planning to do with the milk? Warm it or just drink it straight up?"

"Straight up."

Nodding, he poured two glasses of the cold milk. "Mind if I join you?" he asked.

Amelia gestured to the chairs at the table, thinking it might be a good time to once again extend a hand in friendship. She hoped to help effect a true reconciliation between Ross and Cole.

"Having trouble sleeping?" Cole asked as he put a cold glass of milk in front of her and a plate of cookies between them.

Amelia nodded. "I think I already slept all I'm going to. Ross made me go to bed at eight. Anyway, I woke up and then I started thinking. Dangerous, when you've led the life I have. Do you remember the old song—regrets, I've had a few? That about sums it up for me."

"Come on. Me, maybe, but you?"

Amelia grinned. "I'll match your mistake and raise you two. So, you got sent to military school for going for a joyride in a cop car. Your father knew you were in Virginia at school. I disappeared for four years. Kids. They don't make a lot of sense. I know I didn't," Amelia said and went on to tell Cole why she had run away and how she'd wound up living on the streets of Atlanta.

It was the story of a young girl from a small college town in Georgia, whose brother was a Marine traveling the world. She'd dreamed of becoming a famous photographer and doing the same. But her mother wanted her daughter to study for a career she could rely on.

The girl rebelled and ran away when her mother took away her camera because her grades had fallen. At first she lived on the streets, hiding from the police and begging for food. Finally she managed to find a waitress job and a room, but not before some really scary times.

By the time four years had passed and she was twenty, she'd gotten her high school diploma, a better job and had an apartment and a camera. But she was lonely and she missed her family who, she was sure, had suffered greatly for her actions. She just didn't know how to go home.

She did finally go home, but it took a tragedy. She heard that over two hundred Marines had been killed by a terrorist bomb at the U.S. Marine barracks in Beirut. Her brother's name was on the list of the dead.

So she went home to grieve and to be a comfort to her elderly parents. This time she listened to her mother and trained for a career she could rely on, but ultimately she followed the path where her heart led her.

Cole opened up as he never had before. He told her all the crazy things he'd done before his arrest. He'd wanted to go to jail to shame his father and still didn't know what he'd thought it would prove. But his father had worked a deal to send him to military school, circumventing the jail sentence, and Cole had been furious, threatening to kill Ross if he ever saw him again.

But he had seen what his actions had done to the rest of his family. For the first time, he'd tried to change once at the school. But then Granny Taggert had died, and Ross had waited until after she was buried to notify him. Cole was once again on the road to self-destruction. A teacher had made him his pet project then. He'd shown Cole that he wasn't hurting his father as much as he was hurting himself.

"So do you think you can sleep now?" Cole asked and yawned.

Amelia sighed and let her shoulders slump just a bit. "I don't know. I'm so confused. I thought you liked me, but you're angry with Ross because he's beginning to have feelings for me. What I don't get is why that makes you so angry. How long do you expect him to mourn your mother and punish himself for her death?"

"Mourn my mother? He was about to toss her out of his life. He demanded a divorce the night before she died. I didn't understand it then, but I heard him talking to a lawyer a week later and realized that my grandparents, Mom's parents, had been worth a fortune. A lot more than Dad and Laurel Glen. I figured he'd have gotten half of Mom's money in the divorce and she'd have gotten half his. But two thirds of Laurel Glen was already in trust for Hope and me. She'd have gotten one sixth of Laurel Glen's value out of Dad. He'd have come out of it flush and then some."

"I can't believe that. Ross still worships her. He's never gone on a single date in all these years, according to Meg. Now you sound as if you think he arranged her death."

Cole's eyes widened. "I might have problems

with Dad but I know he's no murderer. For a long time I thought he may have let the horse stomp her for longer than he should have but then I tried to unlock the gun case, load a rifle and get back out to the ring. He was fast that day, and there's no denying he tried to save her. Then I realized she'd ridden the horse because she'd wanted to die. She must have heard me telling Dad the horse was crazy. The rage just exploded, and I stole the cruiser.'' He sighed and slumped in his chair, absently playing with the last cookie. ''The worst part is that now that I'm an adult, I know marriages go sour and it isn't any one person's fault. I know I shouldn't blame him unilaterally. I came home to settle things with him, but the past just keeps getting in the way.''

''Maybe like your thoughts on your parents' marriage, there are other truths you need to discover. For instance, do you know your father asked to be allowed to bring you home for your great-grandmother's funeral? The judge refused. Ross was afraid you'd go AWOL to get there if you knew about it, so he waited to tell you until it was too late. Your father's a good man. So are you. Why can't you two get it together? Think about it!'' She yawned. ''I'm going to bed. The sun's coming up.''

Chapter Ten

Ross woke to the sound of someone pounding on his bedroom door. "Ross. Come quick," Meg shouted. "Georgie's hurt, and the horses have wandered down the drive and out to the road."

He was running down the stairs fully clothed minutes later and didn't even remember getting dressed. Amelia was right behind him, hobbling as fast as crutches could carry her. Cole was behind her. Ross heard her squeal, and turned, thinking she had fallen. Instead Cole had caught her.

"Thanks, Sir Galahad," she quipped.

"Dad, Amelia can call the cops. She's not going to be rounding up the animals with this ankle," Cole said, as if he was in charge of what Amelia could and could not do.

Ross nodded and tore out the front door. He

would have to figure out Cole's attitude later and deal with it.

For the next hour, Ross fought a constant battle to do just that, but it haunted his every action. They rounded up all the horses, then quieted and settled them in their stalls. Georgie was alive and conscious but had seen nothing of his attacker. The older man was on the way to the hospital with Meg following. She wanted to be with the handler who'd been at Laurel Glen since they were both in their teens. By the time everything was settled at Laurel Glen, the police were crawling all over the place.

Ross headed to the house to check on Amelia, who he realized had been left alone in the face of the crisis. He circled the house, headed for the kitchen, and saw Cole by the garage, standing beside his car with Detective Lovell. Cole shook his head and started to walk away when Detective Lovell pulled his gun. Cole froze, a look of incredulity on his face.

Ross took off like a shot. "What do you think you're doing?" he demanded when he reached the two men.

"I'm arresting your son on suspicion of attempted murder," Lovell answered.

Ross's stomach bottomed out. "On what grounds?" he asked.

He'd checked into Lovell, and Amelia had been right-on about the detective. The man wasn't a fool. He was a highly decorated ex-city cop. He'd transferred to the state police after cracking a huge corruption ring in Riverside that led all the way to the office of the police commissioner only weeks away from a mayoral election that the official had been favored to win. The ex-commissioner was cooling his heels in the state penitentiary with a laundry list of convictions on his record.

"It looks as if your handler was hit with the tire iron," Lovell explained and pointed to a blood smeared pipelike object in the back of Cole's SUV. "The tire iron. Your son's car. I've got to assume that's Georgie Burk's blood all over it."

Cole looked pale and badly shaken. He was staring at the tire iron, shaking his head. He looked at Ross. "Dad, I—"

"What time did this happen?" Amelia asked, stepping on whatever Cole had been about to say.

"The handler says it was about four-thirty. He heard a ruckus and went to investigate. Look," Lovell said, glancing at Ross. "I know this is hard, Mr. Taggert. He's your son, after all, but I have to take him in. Maybe we won't find his prints on the iron."

"Of course his fingerprints are on it. It's his. That—"

"Excuse me," Amelia interrupted again—louder this time. "I think I can clear this up very easily. Cole was with me at four-thirty this morning. In fact, he came into the house about three, and he was with me until dawn."

Ross couldn't believe what he was hearing. Amelia and Cole? He'd thought she was so different from Marley. Instead she was exactly the same. That scene of familiarity between them on the stairs earlier made absolute sense now.

"You're sure you didn't fall asleep? Could he have left you and come back?" Lovell asked.

Amelia recoiled. "I don't like your implication, Detective Lovell. We were having milk and cookies in the kitchen. And talking. Men and women still talk occasionally these days. At least they do in my corner of the world."

Lovell grimaced and holstered his weapon. "Sorry to both of you. You'll sign a statement that Dr. Taggert was with you during the time in question?"

"With my hand on the Bible. Cole was with me from three to nearly six-thirty," Amelia asserted.

Lovell nodded and stared at the ground for a long moment, deep in thought. "I really did think the tire iron was too pat. You just don't look that stupid, but it left me no choice."

It was Cole's turn to grimace. "Thanks, I think."

Lovell shrugged and turned away to close the SUV's hatch, handkerchief carefully under his fingertips. "I can only assume that someone's trying to frame you, doctor," he said as he worked. "Any idea who?"

Cole took a quick deep breath and leaned against the rear fender of Ross's 4×4, which was parked next to his. He jammed his hands in his front pockets and frowned, deep in thought. After a few moments, he shook his head. "I hardly know anyone around here anymore. This is really messing up my life. I was going to buy a practice from Doc Brennan, but after you interviewed him following the fire he pulled out of the deal."

It was the first Ross had heard of it. "Cole, why didn't you say something?"

Cole shrugged carelessly, but there was something brewing in his eyes. "I've been on my own for a long time. I've had disappointments before. I'll live." He looked away. "So, detective, now what?"

"The fingerprint team will be up here to dust down your car in case our perp got careless and left prints behind. They'll bag the weapon as evidence. The only thing I can think to do about your situation is put someone undercover out here, but it might be just the slightest bit obvious."

"Those horses out there are more to us than a livelihood," Ross told the detective. "There's not an owner, us included, who wouldn't grieve if something happened to one of them. I don't care if your man shows up in full uniform including the Smokey-the-Bear hat. Someone is out to destroy this family, which is bad enough, but I don't want any more innocent animals suffering because of it. While Georgie was unconscious, they could have started another fire or poisoned every horse out there instead of just turning them all loose, which was bad enough."

"We talked the other day about who would do these things," Amelia said. "Since neither Ross nor Cole can think of anyone who has a grudge against them, we speculated that maybe a developer was trying to drive them out of business."

Lovell shook his head. "I checked on that already. So far I haven't found evidence that anyone has had threats made against them over selling their land. Plus there's a lot of land available for development that hasn't even sold yet. Sorry. It was a great idea, though, Miss Howard. I thought of it myself, so it had to be a great idea." The handsome detective shot Amelia a self-deprecating grin. "If you come up with any more theories, give me a call. And it's Jim. Please."

Ross decided maybe he shouldn't have begun to rethink his opinion of the man, after all. Especially when *Jim* handed Amelia a card she tucked in her pocket.

They decided two officers should come to Laurel Glen. One would know horses and go undercover, supposedly to replace Georgie while he recuperated. Another officer was slated to masquerade as a security guard.

Ross walked Lovell to his car and met the evidence team. Amelia and Cole were still talking when he walked toward the house, but they were in the pergola at the edge of the stone terrace near the kitchen. Seated sideways on one of the padded benches, she had her sprained ankle stretched out in front of her.

She looked innocent and sweet with her head angled back as she looked at Cole, who leaned against one of the colonnades that supported the overhead trellis. Ross wanted to believe her crazy story of cookies and milk in the small hours of the morning in the worst way. But it was a lot to swallow. Had she prettied up a tawdry night for the ears of the officer, or had they really spent all that time just talking? Cole was a good-looking, virile young man, and Amelia was a lovely, beautiful woman. Who could blame either of them for acting on a mutual attraction?

She owed Ross nothing. All he'd done was kiss her a few times, and he certainly hadn't made any promises. As yet he wasn't ready for a next step. Maybe, given his ambiguous feelings, it was time he backed off and gave Cole another chance with the lady. It was a chance Cole obviously wanted. As a father, Ross had failed his son enough. He'd always said he'd make any sacrifice for his children. It looked as if it was his chance to prove he meant what he said. He swallowed and moved forward, his wayward heart heavy.

"You shouldn't lie in your statement when you go in to give it this afternoon, Amelia," he said when she glanced at him.

Amelia looked at him as if he'd lost his mind, and Cole looked as if his heart had just been cut out.

Cole reacted first and quickly. Anger and hurt flared in his eyes. Amelia reached for Cole's arm as if to hold him back, but he threw her hand off with a quick jerk of his elbow.

"Don't waste your breath, Amelia. He was tossing me to the wolves just like I thought. 'Of course his fingerprints are on the weapon. It's his.' I *knew* you believed Lovell. She tried to tell me you only meant it was logical that I'd have touched it, but I know what you really think of me. What I don't understand is how you could think I'd hurt old Georgie. He coached me over my first jump. He snuck me out of the house and sat up with me in the stall all night the night Cobby almost died of colic."

"No," Ross protested. "You've got it all wrong. I believe you were with Amelia and that you're innocent of any of this. I never for a second thought you'd hurt Georgie. Amelia's right. I was only telling Lovell there was a logical explanation for the prints they'd probably find on the iron. You had a flat just after you got here. There was a nail in your tire. Remember?"

"Then what's all this about not wanting Amelia to lie in her statement?"

Ross forced a grin. "Come on, Cole. Your old man's not that far out of the loop. Cookies and milk till dawn? Is that a new code word I haven't heard? Maybe I am out of the loop more than I thought."

Cole looked at Amelia, who was blushing. Then he turned to face Ross. His anger hadn't deflated a bit, though the hurt, wounded look was gone from his eyes.

"Yeah, Dad. It's a code word, all right! Quick of you to tweak to that. It was a hot night last night, I'll tell you. Too bad you slept through it!"

Cole turned and stormed off but only got about ten feet before a whip-cracking voice froze him in his place and turned him around. Ross looked from Cole's thunderstruck expression and turned his surely dumbfounded face toward Amelia. An Amelia he doubted either of them had seen before. Her eyes had gone dark, deep gray, and her jaw looked as if it had been cast in concrete.

"Cole James Taggert," she barked, "how *dare* you impugn my good name. And risk my reputation. And worse, use our friendship in this stupid war against your father. You will apologize right now for that salacious whopper you just told, then you will set the record straight with your father. Then…then you can just go to your room and think about how lucky you are to at least have one parent alive and well."

Ross somehow kept a straight face while his son stammered his way through an apology, hesitated, then shrugging with a helpless grin on his face apparently went off to his room. To think.

Ross snickered when the back door shut behind his son. It was apparently not his first major mistake of the day.

"What are you laughing about, sir! How could

you think I'd let you kiss me the way I did then turn around and sleep with your son? I am appalled by your behavior and your dirty little thoughts. Maybe you are out of the loop! And I'm here to tell you which one. The loop I live in values integrity and morals and prides itself on accountability to the Lord.

"And it values truth! I told you I'd come to care for you, although right now I can't imagine what I ever saw in you, and you can still think I'd betray you and my Lord that way?"

She wasn't the only one who was appalled. He'd done it again. He'd let Marley's actions poison his present and quite possibly the future with Amelia he was beginning to hope they could move toward. This was more than attraction. There was something so different and special about her. And though her anger had surprised him, and though he'd felt the sharp edge of her sweet Southern tongue—an edge he hadn't known existed—he still wanted that nebulous chance of a future for them.

"Don't give up on me," he begged. "As you pointed out, Cole and I are an awful lot alike. We both process hurt into anger and we both shoot off our stupid mouths when we're hurt or angry. I may be an old dog but I can surely learn a few new tricks. Forgive me. I won't waste the chance if you'll let me try to make this up to you."

"You want a chance to make it up to me?" Amelia asked, blinking her liquid, sky-gray eyes a little too quickly. And her sweet, caressing voice had caught in the middle of her question, too. It didn't take a genius to see she was fighting tears. Knowing he'd made her cry tore at Ross's heart. At that moment, he would have done anything to repair the damage he'd done.

Little did he know, when he told her he'd do anything to make it up to her, she'd ask of him what nearly amounted to the ultimate sacrifice.

"If I stay to do the research for the second book I've proposed, I should need the better part of a month. For the rest of my time here, I want you to accompany me to church whenever I go. I want you to reconnect with a place and a loop where a midnight tryst with a man's son would not be taken so lightly as you just did."

Ross shook his head. "No. I didn't take it lightly," he countered. He couldn't let her think he'd sunk that low. "The idea of you with Cole made my blood boil and nearly tore my heart out. But, Amelia, I've done so many things wrong with that son of mine and I didn't want to stand in his way if being with you gave him a little happiness."

Amelia was tempted to accept his explanation. He did quite obviously have feelings for her. His jealousy caused a shameful little thrill, knowing she could drive an otherwise rational man to irrational thoughts. But the thrill was short-lived. A negative emotion, while it might show the depth of someone's feelings, was ultimately a destructive force against feelings of love.

If there was going to be any chance for them to explore their feelings and attraction for each other, Ross had to confront the cause of that negative emotion and seek healing. She didn't intend to risk her heart further with his irrational thoughts festering inside him. While she knew her unconditional love would go a long way in helping him heal, she also knew it wouldn't be enough. Amelia knew herself well. If she let him get closer, if she gave him her heart and he abused it, she would survive, but not whole and unscathed. It already might be too late.

There was only one place for Ross to find the healing he needed in full measure. That place was at the feet of the Lord he was so angry with. But she didn't want to create more resentment against God by trying to force a reconciliation, either. She had to be very careful about that.

"God is a vital part of me and my life, Ross. I'm not demanding you make Him that important to you," she said, hoping to create an atmosphere where he wouldn't go all stubborn on her and harden his heart against the call of the Lord. "But I need you to at least understand why He is important to me and how my faith has caused me to live. Will you go to church with me?"

Ross nodded and dragged a chair over. He sat with his knees practically touching her hip. "I can't promise to like it," he said, "but I'll go see what the big deal is about this church you all go to."

He already didn't understand. "It isn't the Tabernacle or Jim Dillon or religion. I've gone to any number of different churches all over the world, and the one link between them is the peace I feel in God's house. It's knowing Him as a living being. It's all about Him and nothing whatever to do with the people who serve him or the churches themselves."

Ross took her hand. He stared at it and ran a lazy fingertip over the back, then took it fully in his. He looked up, his blue eyes solemn. "I made you cry. You hid it, but I know it was only anger and pride that helped you keep it inside."

"It would help if I understood why you thought what you did. And there are some things I learned talking with Cole last night that you need to hear. The most important is that he knows you asked Marley for a divorce. I need to understand that, too."

Ross stared at her. "I didn't ask for a divorce. Marley did. She said she didn't need me anymore. She had her parents' money and someone else— someone she was having an affair with. She intended to marry him as soon as she was free of me. He apparently had the time to devote to her the way I no longer could since my dad died. She said if I fought her on the divorce or for any of the money, she'd take my kids with her. She said she'd tie me up in family court over custody so long I'd lose either them or Laurel Glen—maybe both.''

''You had no notion she was that unhappy? The children didn't, either?''

''Not a clue. And thank goodness the kids were as much in the dark as I was. And she was killed the next day so they never had to know that she wasn't what we thought. She was apparently a chameleon. Quietly, after the funeral, I talked to her friends. Everyone had a different view of her and none of them jibed completely with the woman I thought I knew. I saw that she was spoiled. I spoiled her. Her parents did, too. We liked giving her the things she wanted and doing things for her because she rewarded us with pretty smiles and she doled out doses of the sweetest affection known to man. We'd all have done anything just to have her bestow her golden touch on us. She was the drug, and we were the addicts.

''Then it all fell apart. It took her less than twelve hours to destroy my world. Cole's. Hope's. Even Meg's, really, though Meg says she was ready to come home.'' He looked away, but not before she saw a terrible fear in his eyes.

''What is it?''

''I'm still so afraid I let her die.''

''You didn't. Even Cole knows that. The financial convenience her death was for you apparently did bother him. He tried a reenactment early on the night he was arrested. He admits he doesn't know how you managed to put that horse down as fast as you did. But he thinks Marley wanted to die because she used a horse she knew wasn't stable and that you drove her to her death by demanding a divorce. Ross, you have to tell him she was the one who asked for the divorce he overheard you two fighting about.''

Ross shook his head. ''No way. Neither of my kids are going to know. I protected them all these years. I'm not destroying the fantasy now.''

''But Ross, what about your relationship with Cole? He needs you. Not a dead mother's false memory preserved for him. What good has it done him so far?''

Ross shook his head, tears in his eyes. ''I promised her. She was still conscious, and I promised. She said she was sorry. That she was just tired of the same old life she'd always had. And tired of pretending to be happy. She said she'd wanted adventure and adoration. The other man gave her that, and I didn't. She just wanted to be free and happy again. I never even knew she wasn't, so in a way Cole's right. I did drive her to do what she did by my neglect.''

''How could you know what she was apparently unable to let you see? Ross, she had a psychological problem. She hid it well but she was sick. Instead of seeking help, she sought escape. That's what the other man was. She didn't know how to tell you, so she planned to run.''

"I don't know about any of that, but I won't hurt Cole and Hope that way or break my promise to Marley. That's the way it has to be. Promise me you won't tell him."

It was hard to watch someone you love making a mistake, but he'd told her what he had in confidence. "All right," she conceded. "I won't say anything, but promise me you'll think about it. Cole needs you, and Marley's lies stand between you."

He gave her a sad half smile. "I promise to think about it," he said, his deep sapphire eyes focused on her face. Then he touched her cheek for a second, and the sadness faded. He knocked the trademark straw hat off his forehead and stared at her with a lighthearted glint in his eyes.

"What?" she asked.

His little smile turned to a teasing grin that became a snicker. "Amelia, you sent my thirty-year-old son to his room!"

Chapter Eleven

Amelia blinked. She *had* sent Cole to his room, hadn't she? She shot Ross a confident grin and tried to cover her embarrassment. She didn't lose her temper often, but when she did—look out! "He, uh, seemed to realize he deserved it. Besides..." She shrugged. "I left him at the kitchen table at dawn. I doubt he ever got to sleep. I know I barely had my head on the pillow when Meg's shouting woke me. He needed some sleep."

"That'll be his excuse for going, that's for sure. So tell me, how did you manage to get Cole to finally open up?"

"By letting him know he wasn't the only one who'd made mistakes in his teens. I told him about myself, so I guess I'd better tell you what a rebel I was back then."

Ross chuckled. "A real wild girl, I bet."

"No. I'm serious. I ran away from home when I was sixteen, Ross. I didn't go back for four years."

Ross's eyes widened. "Your parents must have been frantic. The idea of any sixteen-year-old, let alone a girl, out there alone in the world scares me silly."

"It should. I did things to survive that I'm not proud of, but I did survive, and I went on to better things."

She continued her tale, telling him what she'd told Cole the night before and a bit more about her near breakdown, since Ross was interested in the adult Amelia. He said nothing until she finished her story.

"I knew there was something about your photography or school that bothered you. Didn't your mother ever accept what you do?"

"Not really, but by then she'd been diagnosed with Alzheimer's disease. She told herself and anyone who would listen that I was a famous psychologist who wrote books."

"She was proud of you. That's what you need to focus on. Does it really matter that she confused the reason?"

Amelia shrugged. "I still felt like a fraud every time I went to see her."

"What about your father?" he asked, still holding her hand. "Did he accept your decision to chuck the degree and do what you needed to do?"

"Daddy supported me in my decision. What was so sad about my running away was that Mom would have, too. But I didn't realize that. When she took my camera, I freaked as only an angry sixteen-year-old can. I packed my clothes and caught the first bus to Atlanta. I couldn't see how slim my chance of succeeding in an arts field was. All I could see was that she had no faith in me. She took the camera because I was neglecting all my other subjects. And I was. She never said I couldn't take photography as a minor in college. She just wanted me to have a career to fall back on.

"When I went home, she still insisted I major in something else, but that time I heard what she was trying to say. She and Daddy were older parents, and she knew they wouldn't be around long to help me. Mother thought psychology was something I'd be good at and that it would be a stable career. Intellectually I was good at it but emotionally I couldn't leave the patients behind when I went home."

He kissed her knuckles and smiled. "That explains how you can see the problems between me and Cole so clearly. And how you get people to talk."

"It's also how I know you need to tell Cole the truth about Marley. What if he finds out from someone else?"

"No one else knows. You know, you worry too much. Today, I want you to forget about Cole and me and this nutcase after us. Get some rest. You've had a tough couple days, and this one's only a few hours old.''

There was something wrong with Ross's logic about not telling Cole about his mother's plans, but Ross wiped away her worried thoughts when he scooped her out of the bench and carried her toward the kitchen door.

"What are you doing?" she yelped, though she enjoyed the feel of his strong arms and hard, muscled chest. Ross Taggert was quite a man.

"Cole's ahead of me in chivalry points. Sir Galahad, huh? Then who am I?"

She kissed him on the cheek, enjoying his nearness. "King Arthur, of course." She gestured toward the rest of Laurel Glen. "And this is your kingdom."

I wish it was Monday, Ross thought as he walked out of his room. But it wasn't. It was Sunday, and he'd promised to go to church with Amelia. She was being ridiculous, of course. He wasn't a complete heathen! He believed in God. He just wasn't talking to Him. And he really didn't see what good going to church with her was going to do. Considering his offense against her, though, it had seemed fair at the time. Now it just felt like a badly fitting suit.

Uncomfortable.

But a promise was a promise. Still, Ross walked into the breakfast room feeling like a man on his way to an execution—his own.

Cole looked up from his paper. "Where are you headed all dressed up?" his son asked.

"Church," Ross growled.

Cole blinked, a look of total disbelief crossing his face. "Excuse me? I thought you said church."

"I did."

Cole's eyes widened. "I don't believe it. You're letting Amelia drag you to church? Have you lost your mind?"

The kid acted as if he himself hadn't marched off to his room in the face of Amelia's considerable wrath! Ross snickered, remembering Cole's face when that voice had come out of Amelia's sweet mouth. "You let her send you to your room, hotshot. I wouldn't talk." That wiped the smirk off the kid's face.

"I only went because—"

"Yeah. Whatever."

"Boys, if you two go at it and ruin my breakfast," Meg said, "I swear I'll make sure Ruth Ann burns yours."

Ross made a hands-off gesture and sat at the head of the table just as Amelia came in looking as fresh as a spring morning and just as pretty. She had on a pale green dress that looked like a long T-shirt except it was belted at the waist. Suddenly going to church didn't seem so bad as long as he was going with Amelia.

He still felt okay about it when he pulled into a spot in the Tabernacle's extensive lot. "I can't believe this is a church,'' Ross said, looking at the building for only the third time, though it was where his sister and daughter had worshiped for over five years. ''An old barn, for cryin' out loud. Who puts a church in a barn?''

''Well, Jesus was born in one, if you think about it,'' Amelia countered.

Ross chuckled. ''Good point. The first time I saw it was the night of Hope's wedding rehearsal. It was a pleasant surprise and so was the guy who runs this place. Apparently he thought up renovating the barn instead of tearing it down.''

Amelia laughed. ''Jim Dillon wouldn't exactly agree that he runs the Tabernacle. He'd tell you God runs it through him and his board. For instance, if anyone proposes an idea for the church that will cost money, Pastor Jim feels if it's the Lord's will, the money will turn up.''

''How does the guy get anything done?'' Ross asked, then grabbed her crutches and circled the car to open Amelia's door.

''Simple. He follows the Lord's will,'' she said, putting her hand in his and letting him help her out and steady her. ''The first week I came here,'' she went on, ''Pastor Jim proposed expanding the children's video library. By the next week, an older couple had decided to donate money for the children. The couple had been on vacation, so they had no idea Pastor Jim had mentioned videos for the children.''

Ross nodded, understanding Jim Dillon's principle but not necessarily liking the implication. He thought it sounded spooky.

"Ross, you're frowning. Was it something I said?"

He rubbed the back of his neck trying to loosen the suddenly tight muscles. Why was he letting this place get to him? They weren't even inside yet. "It seems to me if God didn't save Marley, it's pretty lousy of Him to concern Himself with a bunch of videos," Ross replied honestly.

"God didn't cause Marley's death. You know that, I hope."

"That isn't the point. He could have helped."

Amelia looked a little sad as they neared the front door of the church. There goes any chance of sneaking in, Ross thought when he noticed Jim Dillon standing outside.

The young pastor's eyes widened when he saw Amelia on crutches. "What did you do to yourself, Amelia?" he asked. "You didn't get your foot stepped on by a horse, did you?"

Amelia smiled sheepishly. "I did all the stepping, pastor. Right into some poor little animal's house. I probably broke all his little furniture, too."

Dillon laughed and turned. "Ross Taggert, isn't it? Hope's father?" He put his hand out, and they shook hands as Ross nodded, confirming his identity. "I thought that was you. You just missed your daughter. She and Jeff were here for the earlier service. He looks better every day.''

Ross smiled. ''Yeah, he does. They were over for dinner last night.''

''How goes the hunt for Hope's replacement at Laurel Glen? Plans for their school seem to be moving right along.''

''Hope's trying to track down this wonder of an ex-eventer from somewhere up in the Pocono Mountains named Charlie or C. J. Larson. Jeff remembered Larson from a few years ago on the eventing circuit.''

Dillon frowned. ''The name sounds familiar. I have a friend who pastors a church up there. I'll ask him if he knows the name.''

''Appreciate it,'' Ross said, and they moved on.

An usher handed them a program as they walked into the rustic but finely finished sanctuary. A band on the raised platform at the front of the church started playing music, and Ross felt as if he'd fallen down a rabbit hole and landed in Wonderland. Within seconds everyone was clapping in time to the music and tapping their feet to it, too. And they were all singing without using hymnals. They knew the words.

This was not like the church his parents had attended. Hope and Jeff's wedding had been a lot more traditional than this. It was apparent that Jim Dillon ran one really weird church. But Ross kind of liked the relaxed atmosphere and the friendly smiles all around him.

He even liked the beginning of Jim Dillon's message. But later he grew uncomfortable again and wondered if Amelia had called ahead and suggested a message aimed at the visitor she'd dragged with her.

"Morning, everybody. If you're wondering what's with your grinning idiot of a pastor this morning, I'll be happy to explain. Thrilled." He sort of snickered. "Tickled pink, actually."

"Tell the people, already," the usher who'd handed Ross the program called, getting a big laugh.

"Yeah. Yeah," Dillon joked with a dismissive gesture. "This isn't a big deal for him—Trent and Maggie have a full house already. And it looks like I'm going to be right behind him. Holly had an ultrasound on Friday, and we got a surprise. It looks as if the Lord decided to help us make up for lost time. The baby turned out not to be *a* little girl, but two of them."

After a round of applause Dillon said a prayer that Ross tuned out, then the pastor opened his Bible. "We're in James today. Four or five books to the left of Revelations, for those of you still unfamiliar with your Bibles. Before I start on the verses, we need to consider James's life and family history. And what a history. He was the brother of Jesus."

The pastor paused for what Ross assumed was dramatic affect then continued with a bemused expression on his face. "Can you imagine being the brother of Jesus? It sounds great, doesn't it? But think again. Jesus—the only perfect kid ever born, and you're following His act your whole life. Talk about your sibling rivalry and mixed feelings. He's a pain in the neck because He does everything right but He's also the best older brother anyone has ever had—literally.

"Then Jesus hits adulthood and starts talking sort of crazy. James actually had to go with his mother and some of the other family members to a synagogue to get Him. They tried to talk Jesus into coming home where they could take care of Him. You see, it was pretty obvious to all of them that He'd gone around the bend. He wouldn't listen, so James let Jesus go off with His crazy friends to tell anyone who'd listen that He was the Messiah. Meanwhile James went on with his life back in Galilee.

"Time passes, and James learns his brother's made so many enemies that the authorities have put him to death. He's got to be pretty broken up about it. You can see that he understands firsthand two things that plague all of us in our lives—guilt and grief.

"So James goes to Jerusalem to comfort his mother and learns that Jesus has risen from the dead. Now he's got to be thinking—excuse me? My brother is *God?* He rose from the *dead?* This is the kid whose sandals I tied together and tripped when

He was ten! And I put a frog in His bed when He was twelve."

The congregation, Ross included, laughed, but then all joking was over. After another thought-provoking pause, Dillon went on in a soft, sobering tone. "James is heartbroken. 'I doubted Him when He said He was the Messiah,' he had to be thinking. 'I wasn't with Him when he was dying for *my* sins.'

"In the history of the world has there been a deeper remorse for anyone to feel than to have grown up with Jesus Christ, the best brother ever, the Messiah, and still be one of those who doubted Him and deserted Him?"

"Well, obviously Jesus forgave James because he was in the upper room on Pentecost and received the Holy Spirit with the Apostles. He then went on to become one of the leaders of the church in Jerusalem. He wrote this letter to teach us how to live. But his *life* may be his greatest lesson. His life shows us that we need to seek forgiveness for trespasses we commit, and it promises forgiveness. But more important, his life tells us to forgive ourselves for those trespasses. James went on, didn't he? And he couldn't have done the things he did in the early church or have had the nerve to write this letter we call an epistle if he'd been carrying a load of guilt."

Uncomfortable with the pastor hitting so close to home, Ross tuned out the rest of what the man had to say. And he had quite a lot to say. Unfortunately, that gave Ross a lot of time to think.

He'd been a new Christian when Marley turned her attention to him. He'd been able to straddle both sides of the fence for a month or two, but Marley took up more and more of his time. He'd skip a service here, a service there, then two, four.

Then his teenage hormones and Marley's willingness tempted him to a place he'd seen as paradise, and church became a place of discomfort and guilt. He left what he told himself was a thing of his childhood behind. He, too, had turned his back on Jesus.

Then Marley had confessed she was expecting a baby—Cole—and they were married. He'd wanted to return to church, but she always had an excuse why that week didn't work for her.

Then his young father died of an aneurysm, and the financial roof had caved in. And like James, Ross let his life get in the way of looking for Jesus. He'd had a child on the way, a wife and grandmother to support and a mountain of tax debt on land that had been in the family for centuries. He'd cut staff down to one handler and filled in for the shortfall by working sixteen hours a day, seven days a week. He never even thought about God or going to church anymore, and Sunday became just another day. When Marley was killed he'd dragged God out of mothballs as someone to blame.

Who, he was left to wonder, had failed whom? Had God failed him or had he failed God? And why had he blamed God, anyway? So he wouldn't feel it had all been his fault? God had been a handy target—someone to point a finger at. Someone he'd spent the previous decade ignoring.

"Ross, are you all right?" Amelia whispered, drawing him out of his troubling thoughts.

He looked around. The congregation was on its feet singing. He nodded. "Just tired," he said and stood.

And he realized he'd told the truth. He was tired. Tired of feeling anger and turmoil and emptiness. He knew if he found the nerve to reach out to Amelia, she could cure a lot of the emptiness, but not all of it. He'd still need help with the anger and turmoil inside him. He just wasn't sure he had the courage to reach out to the One he needed the help from.

Chapter Twelve

Ross put his hands on his hips and glared at Amelia. "How can you possibly trail after me on crutches and take notes?"

Amelia grinned. Sometimes that innocent air of hers really lulled him into a false sense of security. He forgot how determined she could be. This was one of those times, he realized, when she held up a tape recorder.

"Voice activated?" he asked, knowing the answer.

"Of course. So tell me about what you feed the horses."

Ross sighed. He knew when he was beat. He'd gotten her to rest all day yesterday after church, and today. "Come on, I can give you some information before dinner that ought to keep you busy all night. But be careful where you put those crutches. Horses aren't too careful where they heed the call of nature, and crutch tips slip pretty easily.''

"Yes, boss,'' Amelia quipped.

He turned and raised an eyebrow at her, rigidly fighting a smile. "What did you call me?''

"Uh, Ross. Yes, *Ross*.''

"Hmm. That's what I thought.'' He opened the small door to his left. It was a likely place to start. "This is the feed room. In warm weather we feed most of the horses hay, but some, believe it or not, are allergic to hay. They get haylage. It's grass conserved at a stage between hay and silage. Hay and haylage have around a twelve percent protein content. We move them up to a higher protein content by giving them a concentrated feed.'' He dipped his hand in a barrel. "Like this. Whole maize. They get a percentage of this kind of feed when cold weather moves in or if they're getting more exercise than usual.''

"I always just thought they ate what was on their stall floor.''

Ross looked at her, horrified. "Where do people get these ideas? Horses may look hardy, but they're actually very delicate creatures. You have to be careful of everything they eat. You don't want them eating off the floor. We have to figure out how much they should eat and plan their eating around their work.''

"Work?''

"Being ridden is work. If a horse is going to work

heavily, we take his feed away two hours before he's ridden, and if he's to be ridden easily or moderately, we pull the feed an hour prior. When they're to be switched to heavier protein feeds for winter, we do it gradually or they can get colic. Severe colic can kill a horse.''

''Wow. I know one thing this book will be good for. If a kid is asking for a horse, this ought to discourage any but the most determined.''

''There's more. We also have to adjust the feed to the horse's temperament and how they use the fuel you give them. The rule is to double the horse's height in hands and consider it pounds, then subtract a couple pounds or so depending how well he uses his food. Then if you're mixing feed concentrates with the hay, he'd get two-thirds hay and one third concentrate. That's for animals fifteen hands and above. For smaller horses and ponies like Cobby the rules are different because they always get less concentrates. Did I lose you yet?''

Her eyes were wide and a little stunned, then she grinned. ''I got it on tape. You aren't going to discourage me. So what's in all these bins?''

Ross ran off the names of the feed concentrates. When he mentioned salt licks she wanted to see one, wondering why she'd missed them before. They walked into the yard toward stable one, and Ross explained that salt licks weren't bright white blocks but more like dun-colored rocks. He pointed out sevcral salt licks dotted here and there in the yard and nearby paddock.

They were inside stable one on the way to the tack room when he turned and noticed Amelia staring into Cobby's stall. She really had a thing for the little old guy. Of course, he had a real thing for the cob, himself. He could close his eyes and see Cole holding baby Hope in front of him on Cobby's back, both kids smiling broadly.

"I thought you wanted to learn about tack next?" he asked Amelia.

She frowned, and he noticed she had the little recorder at her ear, listening to it. "Ross, you said that little horses and ponies like Cobby don't get as much of the concentrated feed as the bigger horses and that none of them get it in the summer unless they're going to work hard."

"Right. You really were listening," he said, as pleased as always by her interest. "We'll make a horsewoman out of you real quick."

She frowned. "And didn't you say switches in feed have to be gradual?" He nodded, and her frowned deepened. "Ross, then if it's still so hot why does Cobby have a whole bag of those grass nuts on the floor of his stall?"

Ross responded quickly and tossed the bag of feed out of the stall, but he knew just looking at the old pony that it was way too late. That feed had been in there for hours, maybe as long as a day. The damage was already done. His language probably shocked Amelia, but he was angrier than he ever remembered. This was no accident. The police had better find out who was out to destroy Laurel Glen before Ross did. He wanted to get his hands on the coward who would cause an innocent animal this kind of pain just to fulfill his own petty agenda.

Cobby was pulling his leg toward his belly and looking back at his body with an anxious expression. Then he pawed at the ground and tried to lie down, probably to roll. That was what he'd done years ago, and his intestines had twisted. Ross threw himself against Cobby's side and kept him upright.

"Amelia, call Cole." He gritted the words between clenched teeth as he pressed the pony against the wall of his stall. "Tell him we need him out here. Now."

Amelia hesitated. "But Cole isn't supposed to treat the horses until the burns—"

"Cobby was Cole's first horse. If I don't call him and something goes wrong, it would be Granny Taggert's death all over again."

"I'll be right back." Amelia hobbled to the end of the aisle and the phone.

It was around midnight when Ross walked outside and stood at the edge of the front terrace, his shoulder throbbing in time with his heartbeat. Stopping the pony from rolling had aggravated his collarbone injury. He shook his head. If he needed proof of his age, this was it. Time was he'd have been back in full swing by now. Amelia wasn't going to have to worry about him carrying her around again any time soon. For the life of him he didn't know how he was even going to get undressed. He checked his watch, knowing he had to get on up to bed. Ross tried to do that, but he just wasn't ready to let go of the day.

The lights in the barn's clinic blazed in the distance, which meant Cole and Hope were still out there with Cobby. Hope had come over to lend a hand, and he'd left the kids out there together an hour or so ago.

"Still out there?" Amelia asked, hobbling up behind him, her crutches clicking as she moved closer.

He didn't look back. Sometimes she was a little too much of a temptation. Instead he kept looking at his collapsing little kingdom. Some King Arthur he was.

"Yeah, that's them out there. Hope called a few minutes ago. Cobby's going to make it, but Cole won't come in until he's completely over it. So Hope's sticking with them."

"That's nice. I miss my brother all the time." She chuckled, and Ross fought the urge to turn and pull her against him. "At least this time Georgie doesn't have to sneak him out there to sleep with his pony."

Ross laughed and gave up the fight. He turned and hugged her with his good arm. She was soft and warm against his side, and he found himself wanting to keep her there forever. They'd be able to share everything. He closed his eyes and nearly asked God to grant his wish. But God had stopped listening to him a long, long time ago. Dragging his thoughts off the dark parts of the past, he focused on a lighter memory.

"I'll bet Cole wasn't five yet. He looked so cute when I found him the next morning, asleep in the hay with the biggest stuffed animal in history under his arm."

"You found out?"

"Yeah, but why spoil the little guy's fun? I pulled the same thing myself, but I didn't have adult accomplices so I got caught." He winced at the memory. "By Granny Taggert. Whew. Was she mad! Granny on a tear was not a pretty sight."

"Isn't she the tiny little woman in the ninetieth-birthday picture Meg showed me? Ross, if she was five foot tall, I'll eat my Nikon."

"That sweet little old lady smacked me on the shin with her cane a week before she died. She was one mean old woman!"

"And you loved her to pieces. What did you do that last time to deserve her cane?"

"Do?" He looked at her, trying to look outraged and innocent.

"Come on. What deserved the whack?"

Ross felt his face heat and was glad of the darkness. "I cursed."

"Hmm. Got that cane around here anywhere? I could have used it earlier."

He knew she wasn't talking about getting around

on her sprained ankle. "Or you could wash my mouth out with soap. That was a favorite of hers, too. Sorry about the blue language. I assume that's what you mean. I'm going to work on that. I promise."

"Are you going to do that all alone, too?"

Ross let go and stepped back. "You think I have a choice, don't you?"

"Only if you want one. Are you holding back from asking God's help out of resistance to change or guilt?

"I turned my back on Him. Unlike James, who never believed, I made a conscious decision to opt for a different road after I knew Him as Lord of my life."

"He's *your* Father in heaven, too. If my father welcomed me back with open arms after how badly I hurt him, surely God the Father will forgive you if you ask. Wouldn't and haven't you done exactly that with Cole? God the Father sent His son to save sinners, Ross, not the self-righteous. I saw your face in church. Maybe I'm wrong. Maybe it isn't what you want. But I think it is and I know it's what you need. You can't keep going it alone. Especially not with all the pressure you're under."

Ross nodded and slid his arm around her again. He tucked her head beneath his chin and stood there holding her. He thought back to that time in his teens when he'd put God first and about how easy life had been. Even his grief over his mother's death had been easier to bear than when his father died and he didn't have the Lord to comfort him.

He remembered how hollow he'd felt when Marley had begun to lure him away from God to dwell only in the here and now. She'd called it liberating not to have to worry about eternity but just the concerns of the world. And rather than turn back to where he'd come from, he'd turned to Marley to fill the growing void. Pretty soon he'd grown so used to that empty feeling that it became familiar.

There was so much guilt in his heart. He'd not only turned his back on the Lord but he'd essentially deprived his children of a church background, too. He hadn't wanted any reminder of the days before Marley and all he'd given up for her.

He thanked God for sending Meg into their lives. At least Hope had been raised in the church. He'd argued with Meg about it when she'd come home to help him with the kids and Granny. Ross had been adamant until Meg had asked if he wanted Hope to turn out the way Marley had. She'd been talking about the circumstances surrounding their marriage, but his mind had gone to the last night of Marley's life and the confessions and demands she'd made. He'd given in without a whimper.

He knew he'd be forgiven if he asked for forgiveness. He just wasn't sure he deserved it. He didn't even know he'd spoken aloud until Amelia took on his question.

"Remember when Christ was taken in the garden

and Peter followed to the house of the high priest? Peter denied the Lord three times that night, and the Lord forgave him.'' She patted Ross's chest. ''I think God is big enough to forgive you.''

Ross smiled at her ready answer and found himself praying a prayer he'd learned in his teens. It was a prayer of contrition and supplication that lightened the load of guilt he carried. More important, though, he felt the void in his heart fill. He still wanted to be able to welcome Amelia in his life, and he was still determined to save Laurel Glen, he just wasn't alone in his efforts anymore.

Chapter Thirteen

❧

Amelia stood inside the cool stable looking around for Ross. She'd been told he had gone there after they returned an hour ago from an interview and photo shoot he'd helped her with. He was nowhere to be found, however.

She did notice a pretty little horse that wasn't much bigger than Cobby. She was drawn to the stall. The mare's glistening coat was nearly all black but with an undertone of bay that became the primary color wrapping under her body. Her mane and tail were pitch black and every bit as glimmery as her coat. Amelia was surprised by the tail. She'd never seen a horse's tail grow so long it trailed to the ground. The horse was a real little beauty. Little being a relative term, of course.

The stall had a brass plate on it, which meant it had come off a stall in the ill-fated stable four and that the horse was Taggert stock. The plaque read Queen Morgana.

The mare wandered over, and Amelia gingerly reached out to pet her velvety nose. She was only a little bigger than Cobby, after all. "Oh, you aren't so scary, are you?" she whispered.

"Why would you think Queen Morgana would be scary?" A man's voice boomed from just behind Amelia.

She jumped a foot, scaring the poor horse, whose high-pitched whinny and tossing head scared Amelia twice as much as the man had. She whirled to find Donovan, Laurel Glen's foreman, standing there frowning.

"Why do all you men always sneak up on me?"

Donovan's expression evened out, and he shrugged. "I just walked up, Ms. Howard. You were so engrossed in petting Queen Morgana you didn't notice, is all. So why are you afraid of the Morgan?" he asked, and reached out, calming the spooked horse with his touch in seconds. "Why, these are the sweetest breed of horse I've ever seen—every last one."

"I'm not. Specifically," she qualified, watching him work magic on Queen Morgana. She was embarrassed to admit the full truth. The night of the fire she'd boldly gone into the stable to help get the stock out, but even Cobby had been nearly more than she could handle. Since then the idea of trusting a thousand pounds of horse—give or take a hundred or so pounds—with her life didn't sit too well.

This was not good considering that she'd gone and probably fallen for a horseman. Probably? she thought with self-deprecating humor. *Had,* if she were honest with herself.

"Are you afraid of all horses?" he asked.

"I was petting her," she defended, trying to sound casual and not brave. She wasn't supposed to need bravery to pet a...*pet!* She'd get over this stupid fear given enough time. She was sure of it. Marley Taggert certainly hadn't feared them, she thought, trying not to feel competitive with the dead woman. If only she could convince herself it *was* a stupid fear, but Marley was in a grave somewhere because of one of these beasts.

Donovan scratched his head. "You know, you've been here, what? A month? And I've yet to see you ride. Have none of them asked you?"

"I haven't exactly pushed it," Amelia hedged. "And I rode behind Ross the day I got lost."

"Well, as long as you aren't afraid. Ross wouldn't like to hear that. Ain't seen him look at a woman in years like he looks at you." The foreman got a nearly worshipful look on his face. "His wife, now there was a rider. She was comfortable in any saddle on any horse. And she just beamed when she was up there. Not that she wasn't always sweet and smiling with everyone."

Amelia hadn't had that much contact with the

foreman, but he seemed very nice. He was a plain man. He had a kind of down-home charm, so she refrained from pointing out that Marley hadn't been too happy with her last ride. "I didn't know you were an employee for so long," she said instead.

"I'm here the longest besides old Georgie. He's not the brightest bulb on the tree, so Ross hired me as second in command."

"So you were here when she died? You and Georgie?"

"Yep. Ross and me, we've been through a lot together."

"I suppose he took her death hard," Amelia asked. She didn't know what she wanted to learn about those days, but there was something she needed to know. She didn't know what or why. It was like a faint shadow. Insubstantial and always just out of reach.

"Marley dying the way she did, then Cole turning bad. Tough few years for the boss back then. Yeah, he took it hard. We all did. Some more than others. Ross beat himself up about it. Hate to say it even now, but he was right to. It was his fault. An accident, make no mistake. Not negligence or anything, but he spoiled that boy. A horse like that for a birthday present? He's still too easy on Cole."

Amelia was glad Donovan had never had children if he thought Ross was too soft on Cole. She shook her head. "I think their problems come from each of them having felt guilty over her death. That Cole felt Ross was also at fault in Marley's death complicated things further. They didn't know how to face themselves or each other with those feelings so they showed only anger. Now I think it's mostly habit.''

"Well, whatever it is, it's gonna break Ross's heart to learn it was Cole doing the mischief all along.''

Amelia blinked. Hadn't Ross told his foreman? "But Cole was cleared. He had an alibi the other night. Didn't you hear?''

Donovan frowned. "Been off a few days. But I saw them fingerprintin' Cole's truck Friday. I thought they—I was afraid they'd be out here to arrest him any time now. How could he have an alibi? Old Georgie was attacked when the whole house was asleep. Four-thirty in the morning, wasn't it?''

"Cole's been cleared, Mr. Donovan. They were checking his car to see if the real attacker, who clearly is out to frame Cole, left prints. I was Cole's alibi. You see, we were in the kitchen talking when Georgie was attacked. I couldn't sleep. Cole came in when I was in the kitchen struggling with a milk bottle. We sat down and talked by the light of a candle.''

"Sounds kinda romantic. How did Ross feel about that? I thought you and him were getting cozy. 'Sides, you're a little old for the boy, pardon my saying.''

Men! Even the sweetest of them had a foot in the gutter. "It wasn't romantic in the least, Mr. Donovan," Amelia snapped. "Cole is a troubled person, and I was just listening."

Donovan had the good grace to look embarrassed as he nodded sadly. "He is troubled. That's for sure. The boy's been off since his momma died. He could have hired someone to do all this mischief, you know. Cops think of that?"

She knew everyone wanted this solved, but Donovan seemed to want Cole to be the guilty party. "The police detective thought it was a little too pat, he called it, that the tire iron was in Cole's car in plain sight. It's not Cole doing these awful things."

The foreman sighed with obvious relief. "I sure hope not. Be a shame. A crying shame. And like I said it'd break Ross's heart. He's had enough heartbreak."

"Yes," Amelia agreed. "He certainly has."

Donovan smiled. "So, now that you're done changing the subject, we have to get Ross to let you ride little Queeny."

Oh, no. No way. She'd only just worked herself up to petting one of these oversized eating machines. "I wouldn't want to waste his time like that," she hedged.

"Waste whose time like what?" Ross asked behind her.

Once again Amelia jumped a foot and unsettled the poor horse. Amelia whirled to face Ross. "Will you stop sneaking up on me!'' she shouted and felt immediate contrition. Putting a hand over her heart, she took a deep breath. My, she was jumpy. ''Sorry. I just didn't know you were there.''

''Amelia, if being here while all these problems are happening has you too spooked, you can stay with Hope and Jeff. I could get over there to see you pretty often,'' Ross said.

''I don't think our resident terrorist is her particular problem,'' Donovan said, chuckling, his smile having grown to Cheshire cat proportions.

She knew—she just knew—he was going to suggest she ride Queeny, and she had learned enough since arriving to know a horse could tell you were afraid, and that wasn't good. ''If you gentlemen will excuse me, I'm going to—'' And that was when her mind simply went blank, because Ross was suddenly in front of her and looking worried. He knew very well that she had followed him to get more information for the children's books. ''Amelia, something *is* wrong. What? Please tell me.''

''She doesn't want to bother us,'' Donovan offered. ''Do you know she's been here a whole month and none of us have offered to let her ride one of the horses.''

''You want to ride Queeny? Why didn't you say so?'' Ross asked. ''I'll bet your ankle's strong enough for a little light riding. Donovan, would you see to it the feed gets pulled on Golden Boy and Queen Morgana at about eleven? We'll get Ruth

Ann to pack a lunch and go for a ride and a picnic. There's a little piece of land I'd like to show you.''

"Sure thing, Ross," the tattletale foreman said with a chuckle.

Amelia was tempted to stick her tongue out at him. Instead she took a deep breath and prepared to confess her inadequacy and to see annoyance or disgust on Ross's face. She was no Marley Taggert.

"Uh, Ross. Actually it's not fine. Remember the other day when we rode double back here from my little walk in the woods? Well, that's actually the first time I've ever been on a horse. Except the carousel variety. I have lots of that kind of experience."

Ross didn't frown. He didn't scowl. He didn't even look disgusted. He laughed. A deep belly laugh that had him wiping his eyes and leaning against the stall for support. After a few minutes she was no longer relieved. She crossed her arms to wait out the hilarity. When he didn't get the message that he was treading a thin line, she stalked off. At least as well as someone with a pronounced limp could stalk!

He easily caught up with her in the yard. "Thought we were supposed to check out the tack room," he said as he fell into step next to her.

"Oh, go check it out yourself!" she snapped. Laugh at her, would he?

"Amelia, I know what the tack room looks like," he said, his voice so quiet she could hardly hear him. "You're the one who wanted to learn about it and how much of it the kids helped with.'' He was suddenly in front of her, walking backward and reaching out to cup her shoulders in his big hands. He slowed her to a stop. ''What I want to know is why you never said you were afraid of the animals.''

''Who says I'm afraid?'' she asked coolly.

''Donovan. He thinks they scare you to death, and he's too experienced to miss that kind of fear. So am I, now that I'm looking for it and not just looking at you. My only excuse is that I wasn't eyeing you up as a potential rider the way he was.''

''I was petting that Morgan horse. You saw me,'' she protested.

''And shaking in your boots while doing it. I saw the way you jumped when I came up behind you.''

Amelia sighed. If he was going to be disappointed in her, she may as well get it over with. She'd survived more in her lifetime. ''I'm sorry. I wasn't afraid when I got here, honestly. I've been around horses before, though I've never ridden. I photographed them in action at a string of rodeos earlier in the year. But the night of the fire, I couldn't even control Cobby. That one horse nearly killed Meg. I saw it. And you got kicked, and it broke your collarbone.''

Ross wondered why she seemed so worried about him being disappointed. It wasn't as if it would make a difference to how he felt about her. He tucked her under his arm and steered her toward the practice ring.

"Amelia, those animals were in a panic. Nothing fills an animal with fear quicker than fire. They have a natural instinct to flee to somewhere safe. They think their stalls are safe, just like a child hiding under the bed or in a closet during a fire. We were dragging them out of safety into what they saw as danger. There's not a horse on this place that would hurt a human being normally."

"But they were still all too big to control."

"We don't control them with brute strength but by training and loyalty. I wouldn't have a horse on this farm who was a safety risk. Not after what happened to Marley. I turn away owners who want me to help with a problem horse if aggression toward humans is one of the problems."

He opened the gate into the practice ring and walked her to the ring entrance of stable two. "Here. I want to show you something," he told her as he opened the smaller of the doors—the one meant for humans. It was at the corner of the building. As they stepped inside he let her go, then opened the narrow upright cabinet in the shadowed corner next to the door. He pulled out the rifle that was always there. "There's a rifle like this one at the same place in each stable. Nothing is more important to me than safety. Okay?"

"Okay."

He showed her the intricate lock and where they

kept the cylindrical key hidden. "Every person working at Laurel Glen has a key on their person, and we hide one here just in case."

He let go of her and put the rifle back. "Now I have a tougher question. Do you want to learn or are you too afraid?"

Amelia thought for a moment. "I want to learn. This is your world. I want to understand it. Besides, I hate being afraid of anything, and learning how to ride should get rid of the fear. It always has before."

Ross grinned. She had courage to spare. He liked that about Amelia. But not as much as he liked her generous heart. Then he thought of the way she'd worded her reply.

"Then what do you say I saddle up a nice, gentle horse and we have ourselves a little lesson?"

"Could it be a nice, gentle, *little* horse?" she wanted to know.

Ross chuckled and walked to Queen Morgana's stall. A small whinny echoed into the walkway. "Cobby's out of commission for a few days, but Queen's gentle as they come."

Amelia nodded and smiled nervously. "So what do I learn first?"

"I start the kids with saddling, but I think we should learn that later."

"I thought she couldn't have food so soon before being ridden," she said.

"She's just walking around the ring, not galloping off into the sunset with you."

"You're sure about that?" she asked and tilted her head, shooting him an impish grin.

He wanted to kiss her senseless right there and then, but he'd learned the hard way he should get to know a person—heart and soul—before letting physical attraction get too far ahead of his self-control. There were just too many questions about a woman a man didn't want answered too late. He'd already learned a lot of those answers about Amelia Howard, and so far he liked every last one of them. But this time he had to be sure—even if it meant prolonging this limbolike existence while they slowly explored the possibility of a lasting relationship.

"Relax, Amelia," he ordered. "I learned how to feed a horse by the time I was twelve so I'm sure she's fine, and Queen won't go galloping off into the sunset or anywhere else. She's well trained."

"Just checking," she assured him as he led Queen Morgana, already saddled, out of her stall. "You were pretty sure of your persuasive powers, Mr. Taggert."

He shook his head. "I just had a feeling you wouldn't let a little uncertainty beat you, so I had her saddled. You aren't going to prove me wrong, are you?"

"No. So what do I do? I know I mount on the left side. That's the extent of my knowledge."

"You know more at the start of your first lesson than three-quarters of the students I've taught."

She laughed. "Big deal. I've seen how young you start them, remember?"

Ross took her hand. "Come on," he said and led the horse to the ring with her by his side. He put the reins in her hand when they got there. "The first thing you need to do is put the reins over the horse's head. Keep one on either side of her neck, then holding the reins to the left side put your hand on her neck just in front of the withers. That's the ridge between the shoulder bones."

He stood behind her and cupped her shoulders in his hands so she would know he was right there. He wanted her to deal with Queen Morgana by herself. She had to know she was dealing one on one with the Morgan and that the horse was responding to her and not him.

She looked at him, her eyes more gray than blue today. "Now what?" she asked, clearly apprehensive.

"Now you get on. Just listen to what I say first then we'll go through it again as you do it. Okay?" She nodded and looked away. "This is a Western saddle," he continued. "You'll take down the stirrup that's still over the saddle and put your left foot in it. Then you'll grasp the pommel with your right hand, bounce and swing up into the saddle. Try to sort of ease onto her back. Don't just plunk down. Also be careful not to poke her belly with your toe or kick her hindquarter with the foot you swing over the saddle. Ready to try it?"

She took a deep breath. "As ready as I'll ever be."

"Good girl. Okay—foot in the stirrup, hand on the pommel, bounce, swing, settle easily, right foot in stirrup and stand, keeping your weight on the right foot to straighten the saddle. There! Now that wasn't so hard."

He patted the Morgan on the neck, silently thanking her for her good behavior. Then he looked up at Amelia and knew she was a long way from convinced.

"You were wonderful," he said and took her hand. "Ready to walk a little around the ring?"

She gave him a nervous smile. "I am but I don't know about Queen Morgana here," she quipped.

Chapter Fourteen

Ross watched Amelia lead Queen Morgana across the yard toward him. She looked kind of—what was it she called it—Eastern cowboy today. He watched the subtle sway of her hips and quickly rephrased that—cowgirl. Emphasis on girl. Everything she did, no matter how athletic, she did with a feminine flair.

He nearly laughed when he saw Queen Morgana pluck the Phillies cap he'd bought for Amelia out of her back pocket and happily chomp on it as they traveled toward him.

"How's Queen Morgana today?" Ross asked her, somehow keeping a straight face. Amelia beamed a smile at him that had his heart flopping around in his chest like a trout in a fisherman's net.

"I think she knows my voice now," Amelia answered excitedly. "Cole walked me down to the stable, and when she heard my voice, she stuck her head out of her stall. She was looking for me. And she whinnied when she saw me.''

"She may have just been looking for her next snack. And I'd say she found it," he told her, pointing to the happy chomper.

Amelia turned around. "Oh. You bad girl," she said, anchoring her hands on her hips. "You give me that! This was a present and a memento of my first baseball game." She fearlessly extricated the cap from the horse's mouth, the brim decidedly crumpled. "How could you? It's ruined!"

Ross cleared his throat. "You hide those carrots you've been sneaking her in that same pocket. I bet she was pretty disappointed with the taste of her treat this time."

She looked at the hat and at him, a surprising pout on her lips. "But this was my Phillies hat."

He wanted to kiss those pouting lips in the worst way, but resisted feelings he didn't fully understand. He hadn't kissed her since finding her lost in the woods. His restraint had nothing to do with Hope learning of his attraction to Amelia and everything to do with Amelia and the depth of her feelings for him.

He didn't want to hurt her and he didn't want to be hurt. But Ross didn't feel ready to ask Amelia to share more than a few weeks with him. It wasn't a lack of feelings for her holding him back. He was sure he was coming to love her. He knew he wanted her. But he'd felt love and lust before and been betrayed. He needed to be sure of something he couldn't put his finger on. Perhaps his own judgment, because when he thought of Amelia as he'd come to know her, it couldn't be that he was unsure of her.

"I'll get you another Phillies cap," he told her to distract himself with lighter thoughts. "They're a dime a dozen around here." Ross shot her a teasing grin and patted the Morgan's neck. "And quit trying to act mad at her. Queen Morgana knows a loyal subject when she meets one, don't you, your majesty?"

The horse snorted and tossed her head as if agreeing, making them both laugh.

"You all set to head out?" Ross asked Amelia.

She nodded. "All ready. I'm not very stiff today, either. I guess my muscles are getting in better shape."

Ross was tempted right then and there to rethink teaching her to ride. If her muscles were shaped any better, his self-control would be even more sorely tested. Fighting a smile at his absurd thoughts, Ross checked Queen's girth then, after giving Amelia the go-ahead to mount, checked and climbed into his saddle.

They rode south from the yard, then veered west to a shaded spot where a stream meandered through a large, undeveloped corner of the property. It was a spot he'd decided long ago would remain untouched by anything more than the occasional human on a hunt for time with nature. It was the place he'd chosen to plant a tree in memory of each of his parents and Granny after their deaths. He'd never managed to bring himself to plant one for Marley, and he felt guilty about that, too. Most of the time the only feelings he could recall in relation to his late wife were ones of guilt.

Shaking off gloomy thoughts, Ross dismounted and loosened Golden Boy's girth then did the same for Queen after Amelia slid to the ground.

"I forgot to ask what the emergency was that dragged you away from the breakfast table before you finished your coffee," Amelia said while he spread the picnic blanket.

"A fence was down on Indian Creek Road again. We were going to use that pasture today to get Jeff's stallion and one of my mares together. They'd both have bolted onto the road for sure. Luckily, Hope decided to ride the fence before she turned Mr. March loose."

Amelia looked thoughtful, her sparkling gray eyes narrowed. "That's the fourth bit of vandalism since we found that bag of feed in with Cobby."

"Four in four days." Ross sighed. "I'm getting to a point where I hate to answer a phone. Listen, let's not talk about any of that today. This whole thing is consuming all our time together. It's all any of us seem to talk about."

"This isn't just your livelihood under attack. It's

your home, your past, present and future. Your world. Please. Don't think I mind.''

He let out a frustrated groan. ''Then I need a break from my world. Tell me something about Amelia's world. What's the craziest thing you've done to get a photograph?''

''I guess I blew the whole ladylike image right out the window by taking you on my photo shoots. So I guess telling you I went up in an unfinished skyscraper to get a shot of a bridge at sunset won't shock you.''

Ross blinked and stared at her. Shock? No. Worry? Apparently, yes. And that worry worried him. There was no denying the idea of her in danger filled him with a chilling fear or that the fear brought his emerging feelings into sharper focus. *Why her, Lord? She's not the first female friend of Meg's to visit. Why are all these long-denied feelings suddenly awakening? And with all that's happening, why now?*

''How unfinished was it?'' he asked, surprised that his tone was so even and unaffected by his churning emotions.

''It was still pretty much only I-beams and steel decking at the upper levels. The shot was well worth it. It's in *America the Beautiful*.''

He remembered the photo. Naively he hadn't thought about where she'd stood to take it. ''It was breathtaking,'' he said, and handed her a plate and a napkin. ''Ham and cheese, turkey or tuna salad,'' he told her, pointing to each variety of sandwich Ruth Ann had sent along. Amelia picked up the turkey, and he grabbed one of the same.

"So what's your next project going to be after you finish here?" he asked.

Amelia's head shot up, a look of sadness chasing across her delicate features, then she shrugged but didn't quite bring off the casual air he thought she'd been trying to portray. Ross could have kicked himself. Her leaving was a subject they'd studiously avoided.

"I hadn't thought about it," she said. "I guess I'd better." Amelia looked at her sandwich, still in its wrapper, and put it down as she pushed to her knees. "And speaking of my profession, this is a lovely spot. I think I'll take a few shots."

Ross watched Amelia gather her camera and loop it over her head with mixed emotions. He knew his hesitance about any future for them must hurt her, but if he reached out now only to pull back she'd be doubly hurt.

The trouble was, needing to ease her pain was as strong a desire as his need to protect his heart. He fought the urge to follow her for a good ten minutes then gave up the battle.

It was a shock, even after her skyscraper story, to enter a small clearing about five or six hundred feet west of the stream and see her perched in an ancient oak with her camera focused on something in the distance.

He wanted to yell and scream and shout at her to get back to earth where she was safe, but he was afraid to utter a word lest he startle her. So he stood, heart in his mouth, while she concentrated. She was so intent on her subject she didn't see him until she prepared to descend.

"Hi," she called. "You should see it from up here. Quite a view."

"It's one heck of a view from down here, too," he muttered as he walked across the clearing to the base of the tree. He watched in amazement as she somehow managed to look absolutely elegant while carefully picking her way down the limbs and branches of the old oak. Flushed and dewy from exertion, she was almost more than he could resist when she landed on the ground in front of him.

Laughing, she tilted her head back and looked at him, the look in her eyes nearly daring him to kiss her, but then her smile died and the challenge in her eyes disappeared. She turned away. Ross caught her by the wrist, marveling at the fine-boned delicacy of her strong limbs.

"What did you see?"

"Laurel House. It almost looks like an enchanted castle." She gave a little tug, and he let her go. She smiled at him over her shoulder. "There's a sandwich with my name on it. All that climbing sure worked up an appetite." She hefted her camera. "If they turn out as well as I think they will, I'll make sure to blow up a print for you and Meg."

Ross followed her to the blanket, determined to discover what it was that held him back from reaching out to so incredible a woman.

A shiver chased up Amelia's spine as she stared at the broken lock in her hand. She was safe, she told herself, but she still felt as if she were being watched. She looked about her then to the other end of the stable where Ross stood in the doorway signing for a package.

Everyone's skittish, she told herself. That's all it is. She'd been right. The dirty tricks and arranged accidents were escalating and getting personal. After yesterday's picnic Ross found a hat pin embedded in the pad of Queen Morgana's saddle. Only luck had kept the pin from sticking and spooking the Morgan. Another had turned up while he saddled the horse of one of the young riders.

He'd been casual about it until the child left, then he'd returned to Laurel House. She and Meg had been sharing a glass of tea when he'd stormed through the kitchen and grabbed the phone in the breakfast room. He'd called Detective Lovell, told the man what he'd found then gone without another word to his study.

She'd followed. Just as she'd reached his door a heavy object hit it on the inside, resounding in the hall. She'd backed away, deciding that he might vent his frustrations better without an audience.

Ross wouldn't let her go anywhere without a

companion. He was usually with her, or Meg was. After the picnic, during which Ross had been an odd mix of aloof and attentive, she thought about leaving immediately with her pride intact. But Meg insisted Ross had things to work through, and once he did she would be thankful she'd stayed.

Amelia feared Meg was a little blind where her brother was concerned. Ross had made it pretty clear that while he shared the physical attraction she felt and that he cared for her, he could not take that extra step into love. She was afraid Marley still had him even if it was guilt and not love that held his emotions imprisoned. But with her heart already given to him, Amelia didn't see what more she had to lose by staying.

Dragging her thoughts to the broken lock in her hand and off her breaking heart, she called to Ross. "What's kept in this room?"

He turned away from the delivery man and chuckled, then started toward her. Amelia found herself watching his loose-limbed gait as he strolled down the aisle toward her. For a few enjoyable moments she lost her train of thought, but then he answered her question, and she remembered the broken lock in her hand.

"That's the award room. Meg shipped all the old trophies and ribbons out here when she redid the house a couple of years ago. She said Granny named it Laurel House because it was the house not the farm, so farm awards didn't belong in there."

"The lock's broken."

Ross frowned and reached past her for the lock. "I thought Donovan was overreacting when he put this on. The awards are a matter of record. They don't have any financial value." He slowly pushed the door inward and flipped on the light. He stood motionless, blocking the doorway with his wide shoulders, but Amelia saw a glimpse of the destruction beyond.

"That creep! Oh, I just want to bash him a good one!" she declared, her hand fisted with impotent fury.

Ross turned and raised an eyebrow. "Why, Ms. Howard, how bloodthirsty of you. I'm starting to sound like a broken record. I'd better call nine-one-one. Maybe they should just leave their evidence kit out here. Save them the lugging back and forth."

"Ross, I—"

"Don't," he said and leaned forward to plant a quick peck on her cheek. "I'm sticking to my story. They were just mementos that most of us forgot were even here."

Amelia stepped into the room, and her toe kicked a broken trophy. She picked it up, and Ross took it from her.

"Hope's first place in the Three Day at Devon. She was fifteen. She beat three Olympic hopefuls. She's an incredible rider. But it was the last time she competed."

"Why?"

Ross shook his head and got a wistful look in his eyes. "I asked her that same question. She said— and this is close to a direct quote—'I entered to beat the pants off that supercilious Jeff Carrington and I did. I proved what I set out to prove.'"

"Did it take twelve years for them to kiss and make up?"

Ross raised an expressive eyebrow. "There are some things a parent doesn't want to know." He chuckled. "But I don't think it was a lovers' spat of any kind—not on Jeff's side, anyway. I think she saw him as more, and his brotherly pats on the head got her riled. Hope being young—and being Hope— took great exception to his attitude and got great pleasure out of torturing Jeff in those days. I don't think they stopped spatting until she knocked his brotherly socks off at last year's Valentine's Day dance."

Amelia remembered the sequence of events Meg had explained to her. "And then a week or so later Jeff was crippled in one of the first accidents Laurel Glen's tormentor staged. Right?"

Ross sighed and set the broken trophy on a listing shelf. "It always comes back to that, doesn't it?" He pulled out his cell phone and hit 911.

Chapter Fifteen

Amelia rubbed her eyes and blinked at the screen of her laptop. The articles she'd pulled off the Internet about the trouble at Laurel Glen still swam around in her mind. She checked her watch and blinked, hardly able to believe it was four in the morning. She yawned and shook her head, trying to wake herself, then pulled out the list of clues she'd assembled by talking to Ross, Meg, Cole and Donovan. The attacks, even when directed at the business end of Laurel Glen, were all personal in their own way. Because Laurel Glen was the Taggert family.

Except for Hope. This vendetta hadn't spread to Lavender Hill. It might seem that way because Hope had been hurt when hay bales fell and nearly killed her. But that was the one accident no one could prove had been anything more than an accident. And there was no doubt that Jeff Carrington's fall had been meant for Ross.

Until then the arranged accidents had been impersonal vandalism, but attempted murder had been personal. Very personal. As had the attempt to frame Cole. So who hated both men?

Men?

Cole had been a boy the last time he and Ross had been together. So how could they have made a common enemy?

Amelia yawned and started packing up her computer. No matter how desperate she was to unravel the clues she'd assembled, she still had to sleep. Tomorrow was another day, and maybe with a clearer mind she could find the missing piece of the puzzle.

Knowing she'd never sleep if she didn't get her mind elsewhere, Amelia purposely turned her thoughts from the mystery surrounding Laurel Glen to Ross and all she'd learned about him in the last couple weeks.

He'd taken her into Philadelphia to the Rodin Museum and the Philadelphia Museum of Art. She'd found they shared tastes in art. When they'd enjoyed a Delaware Symphony concert and a seventies revival at the Mann, they'd realized their music tastes were compatible, as well. They differed on literature. Her taste leaned toward romance and other character-driven books, while Ross liked biographies and adventure. When they'd debated the different genres it had been a lively, good-natured exchange.

They both liked to experiment with international foods, too, but only in restaurants, because neither could boil water without scalding the pan. That discovery had led to an incident that served as a warning to Amelia that Ross was determined to deny them a future. He'd been teasing Ruth Ann, saying she probably liked Amelia as much as she did because she wasn't a threat to the cook's job security. It had sounded as if Amelia would be making Laurel House her home, but he had rapidly backpedaled, causing a desperately awkward moment.

Because of the panic his expression had revealed, Amelia felt obligated to finish her work as soon as possible. And it was moving along quickly, though she had learned her publishers liked the children's book idea so much they wanted to make it a four-book set, one representing each season on the farm. She thought they would have to settle for one about summer because she seriously doubted she'd be there in any other season. And she would certainly not return to take seasonal shots and reopen the scars of Ross's rejection.

When all was said and done, she could justify staying less than another week at Laurel Glen. She would simply not hang around waiting for Ross to change his mind about them. Because in his presence she didn't seem able to remain aloof. If her imminent departure or her absence didn't make his heart grow fonder, she faced sure heartbreak.

In the dark, Amelia made her way toward her room from the library, where she'd gone to plug in her modem. She stopped on the landing between the first and second floors, at the window overlooking Laurel Glen. She wanted one last peek at the serene scene of the farm, quiet and asleep under the clear, star-studded sky.

But all was not quiet and right. The security lights were out, and a figure moved furtively in the shadow of stable two. She grew more suspicious when the moon glinted off a shiny head. She knew it couldn't be the state policeman Ross had hired as a night guard, because the officer had a full head of hair. When he slipped in the side door, he stopped and looked around with a wary, cunning stance before closing the door. Amelia felt deep in her bones that he was up to no good.

She hated to wake Ross if there was nothing wrong, and she'd feel like a fool if it was a false alarm, but she'd feel even worse if the person harmed one of the animals in some way. After setting her laptop and other supplies on the landing, Amelia ran as quickly as her tender ankle would allow toward Ross's room.

She knocked on his door. "Ross. Ross. Come quickly."

"What's up?" he asked, wearing a pair of jeans

and an open shirt when he opened the door less than a minute later.

"The security lights are off outside the stables, and I saw someone moving around outside stable two. It didn't look like Officer Sentella. He looked as if he was sneaking around instead of patrolling, especially when he went inside. I thought you should know."

"Thanks. Wake Cole, will you? Send him after me. I'm not much good with this busted wing if there's really trouble brewing."

He went to move past her, but she reached out and grabbed his arm. "Shouldn't we call the police?"

"I don't want to cry wolf. They've been out here so much lately I hate to call if nothing's wrong. It'll be okay. Just send Cole."

Amelia nodded and ran down the hall to wake Cole. He came charging out his door, still dressed but bleary-eyed.

"What's wrong?"

"Someone was sneaking around stable two. Ross went down to check it out. He thought he might need your help."

"I'll go check on him," Cole said, then loped away.

Amelia stood alone in the middle of the long hall shaking with fear for Ross. She ran to the landing window in time to see Ross enter the stable. Cole was more than halfway there and running full throttle. But still she couldn't just stand there. If nothing else, she could call the police.

She grabbed her cell phone and headed after the men. She'd almost reached the center door when Amelia remembered the rifles Ross kept just inside the small door to the practice ring of each stable. He'd said they were kept loaded at all times. Amelia ducked inside the fence and moved toward the practice ring door.

It was black as pitch in the shadow of the building so she had no warning when she fell over something on the ground and went sprawling. The warmth of still flesh under her hand sent her skittering away, and she let out an involuntary squeal. It was the state policeman.

No longer in doubt that there was indeed trouble, Amelia dragged the cell phone out of her pocket with trembling hands and dialed.

"Police dispatch," the voice at the other end of phone said.

"My name is Amelia Howard," she whispered. "Send help to Laurel Glen Farm on Indian Creek Road. I just found Officer Sentella unconscious or dead. I can't tell. Mr. Taggert and his son have gone to find the man who did this. They may need help."

"Tell them to wait for the police, ma'am."

"Too late—they're already looking. I have to go help them."

"Ma'am, you'd better stay put."

"I can't! Just send help," she whispered frantically and turned off the cell phone. She didn't need it ringing at the wrong time if she was going inside to try to help. It was too dark to see what was wrong with Sentella so she couldn't help him, but she might be able to help Ross and Cole. And something told her she had no choice but to try.

Creeping to the door of the stable, Amelia tried to settle her breathing. She cracked the door open and slipped inside. Because she'd used the small access door, she was hidden from view by the right side row of stalls.

When she peered around the edge of the first stall, she saw Ross and Cole standing next to each other in profile. A stranger held a gun on them. In the man's other hand was a syringe. The hand shook as he snarled, "Why couldn't you two have stayed in bed like the good little farmers you was supposed to be?"

Cole's posture changed from stiff to a hip-thrusted slouch. "Pal, I haven't been good since my first shave," he quipped in that smart-aleck tone he got when he was feeling unsure or cornered. He was certainly cornered.

"Well, you ain't gonna have to worry about that much longer," the man replied.

"Look," Ross said. "You've done no harm yet tonight, and no one's been permanently hurt before this. If you'll just tell me what you have against us, maybe we can reach some kind of settlement."

The man only laughed. Amelia wished it wasn't

such a nervous laugh. She knew from her psychology work that an anxious person with a gun was more dangerous than one feeling confident.

Her heart tripped over itself when Ross's eyes cut quickly to her and back to the intruder. He knew she was there. She took a slow breath. Keeping her eyes on the frightening tableau before her, she felt for the key then moved out of sight to the rifle case in the corner and gingerly opened it. Finally her fingertips contacted the cool steel of the rifle. She wrapped her fingers firmly around the barrel and carefully lifted it out.

It was long and heavy, and her hands shook. But she'd had to learn to handle a rifle when she went on a photo shoot in Africa two years earlier. She'd never had to fire at a live target, but she'd been a good shot in target practice. To protect Ross and his son, she knew it was all right to use the rifle. She just didn't know if she'd be able to pull the trigger to kill a man.

Please, Father, don't make it necessary, but let me find the strength I need to protect them.

"If you pull that trigger, this barn'll be crawling with witnesses in seconds," Ross warned, making Amelia jump before she realized she wasn't the one he'd spoken to. She only just kept herself from dropping the weapon, and her heart thudded so hard she swore in was banging into her rib cage.

"What are you going to do, shoot everyone on the farm?" Cole added.

"No, but your old man's going to come over here and stick his arm out or I'm going to chance putting a bullet square between your eyes, smart boy."

"Don't move, Cole," Ross ordered when Cole went to rush the assailant.

"Dad, don't let him stick you. I—"

"For once," Ross snapped, "don't argue."

"That's real smart advice, Taggert," the gunman said and brought the gun up, aiming at Cole's head. "Get over here now or sonny boy's going to be history."

"Okay—okay," Ross said, then his eyes flicked to Amelia before he looked up at the big light, high at the peak of the roof. Amelia almost screamed when Ross stepped in front of Cole and into the line of fire from the stranger's handgun.

And this man thinks of himself as a bad father?

"Get back over where you were!" yelled the intruder.

"Listen, would you make up your mind?" Ross grumbled and stepped next to Cole. He was closer to his son. "Come here. Go there. What do you want me to do?"

Ross had thoroughly rattled the man, and Amelia figured if she didn't move now it might be too late. If she shot out the light, the entire stable would be dark. She didn't know what Ross's plan was after that, but she didn't want to second-guess him, either.

Amelia took a final breath, aimed and fired. The glass globe shattered, the gas inside the light flared then darkness fell amid the sound of heavy glass shards hitting the stone floor and horses screaming in fear.

Someone else screamed, as well.

Then silence fell, leaving Amelia standing in the darkness, stunned by what she had seen just as the light blinked out. She started to shake as one by one the older incandescent lights of a bygone era blinked on. Then Ross was there, gathering her into his arms and holding her tight against him. He was so solid and alive, and she felt the opposite.

"You saved our lives, sweetheart. Before you came in, he told us what was in the syringe. Cole said it's what they use to put down horses. He said there was enough there to kill an elephant. After sticking me with it, he'd have shot Cole. I'd never have lived till they got me to a hospital."

Good as it felt to have him hold her, his nearness was not enough to chase away the truth. She couldn't close her eyes and not see the stunned expression on the gunman's face. "I didn't mean to shoot him. I don't know how I did," she whispered, her voice sounding strange to her own ears.

"Your shot must have ricocheted somehow and hit him. How is he?" Ross asked Cole as his footsteps approached.

Amelia turned her head toward where the three men had stood. The man lay behind Cole, who stepped purposely to the right to block her view. His expression was grim, and he shook his head. "He's gone."

The floor tilted, and her head spun. She'd killed a man? "Oh, dear Lord, I'm so sorry," she cried. Half an hour ago she'd been a journalist, and now she was a killer. She took a shuddering breath when another possible death reared in her mind. "The policeman!" she sobbed. "He's in the ring. I called the police after I found him."

"Go check on Sentella. You may be able to help him," Ross said to Cole, keeping Amelia firmly in his arms. Cole nodded and headed for the door.

"When I found him, I knew you were in trouble. I couldn't do anything to help him till I helped you," Amelia said, trying to explain why she hadn't stayed with the officer. Then her thoughts veered to the intruder. "I never meant to kill that man."

"I know, sweetheart. I'm so sorry you were put in this position. No one's going to blame you. All you did was shoot out a light."

"The cop's alive, but he's unconscious. I need some light out there," Cole said as he came in and flipped on the outside lights, which should have been on all along. "And you didn't shoot our intruder, Amelia. Someone at the yard door did. I saw the muzzle flash just as the light blinked out. I asked him what we'd done to make him hate us like this. He shook his head and said 'hired' but not who hired him."

"So it's not over," Ross said, his voice flat with resignation.

Ross opened the kitchen door to Detective Lovell an hour after the police arrived at the farm. Lovell took a seat at the end of the kitchen table, and Ross slid onto the banquette and put his arm around Amelia. He was worried about her. All her wonderful spunk seemed to have drained out of her.

"Okay. Here's what we've got so far," Lovell said. "The intruder was killed by a second gun," he told them. "You weren't alone out there. We didn't find a single clue as to who it might have been, but we found a shell casing, and the shot was fired by a different-caliber rifle."

He looked at Cole. "You were right, the drug locker in the barn was broken into, so we can't trace the purchase.

"And Officer Sentella is going to be fine. He'll have one miserable headache tomorrow, but that ought to remind him not to be so careless. When he noticed the yard lights out, he should have been suspicious. Ms. Howard certainly was."

Ross squeezed Amelia's shoulder. "See, Cole was right. You didn't hurt anyone and you saved lives. Cole's, mine and the horses'." He was afraid she was in shock when he got only a nearly imperceptible nod in answer. He wanted to get his hands on whoever had hired the dead man. That person had put Amelia in a position no person, let alone a sensitive woman, should be placed in.

Ross looked across the table at Cole. As upset for her as Ross was, he couldn't wish Amelia hadn't been there. His son was alive because she'd followed them. He was grateful to her and he felt a terrible load of guilt over her need to rescue them.

"What confuses me," Lovell continued, "is why the second gunman held his fire and didn't kill one or both of you instead of his accomplice."

"I think we're in agreement that being alive is worth the confusion," Cole drawled.

Lovell grimaced. "What I meant was, what does this guy want if not to kill you?"

"To destroy us slowly," Ross said and fought a shiver that moved up his spine when his words sparked a terrible thought.

"My point exactly. This guy's enjoying this," Lovell retorted. "He was willing to kill, which means he didn't hold off tonight because he won't go that far. He obviously killed our perp to keep himself from being identified. So why did he want you two alive? It has to be that he's getting satisfaction out of watching you both lose everything you care about. Our job now is to figure out who could have such a deep grudge against you two that he'd find pleasure in prolonging your agony when he had you in his sights."

Ross shook his head. "I don't have a clue."

"Well, we have to come up with something, and

soon. He came close to being exposed tonight. He's either going to escalate or fade away and strike again when you least expect it.''

Cole nodded. ''There was enough drug in that syringe and the second one they found on his body to kill every horse in that stable. That would have killed Laurel Glen as a business. Plus, it came from my drug cabinet, so he's not done trying to frame me. And the second shooter did have plenty of time to kill us if he was lurking out there in the dark.''

Since they all agreed with Lovell they went over the scene in the stable once again, trying to recall any clues they might have missed. Then they went over it again. And again. But nothing new came to light, and Amelia drifted off to sleep on Ross's shoulder.

He was worried about her. She hadn't added a thing to the speculation, which was unlike her and her quick mind.

A couple of hours later the crime teams left Laurel Glen, and Lovell suggested they all try to get some sleep. Ross carried Amelia to her room in spite of his aching shoulder and left her in Meg's care. He hated leaving her alone and vulnerable to the bad memories the night had given her but he had no right to stay.

None at all. And Ross doubted he ever would.

He stood outside her door and prayed the Lord would hold her in His hand till she woke. Then, feeling about a hundred years old, he nearly staggered to his room to prepare and pray for the day ahead. Because his mind was made up. He had to send Amelia away where she'd be safe.

So far he'd been lucky. If whoever was out there realized how much she meant to him, she might become a target. And he couldn't lose her like that. He remembered holding Marley, trampled and broken, in his arms as the life drained out of her. Then there was the terror he'd experienced when he'd realized Hope lay unconscious beneath hundreds of pounds of hay with Jeff's already injured back the only buffer. There were some things that were too much to endure. At least this way Ross would know Amelia was out there somewhere healthy and happy. And safe.

As for a future for them, he'd come to a realization as he carried Amelia to her room. Cole had suggested he take her up, but Ross, feeling possessive and protective, had eschewed the offer. But as he neared the second floor, he remembered carrying Marley up that same staircase feeling lighter than air—not weighted down by too many years and too many weighty issues sitting on his shoulders.

Amelia had as much as said his age didn't matter, but suddenly on top of everything else he knew it did. She was too young for him, or rather it was really a case of his being too old for her.

It was an impediment he'd chosen to ignore weeks ago, but he wondered what he'd been playing at. He had eleven years on her. Ross knew she wanted children. He'd acknowledged that he wouldn't mind more himself. Maybe he'd have gotten it right this time, having learned from his mistakes. But he saw that for the delusion it was. He'd be in his sixties with teenagers to deal with. If they married and had that mythical child immediately he'd be in his seventies when their oldest child graduated college. What had he been thinking?

He didn't want to hurt Amelia. He was sorry he'd gotten so caught up in getting to know her that he'd probably given off mixed signals that at least promised a chance for a future for them. But surely once she left here and got back to her exciting life, in the company of younger men, she, too, would see how foolish they'd both been.

He'd also decided to send the horses to other stables. He hoped his clients would respect his decision to keep their animals safe at all costs. Perhaps they'd return them after this was all over.

If it was ever over. Lovell's warning about their tormentor going underground and surfacing when it was least expected was nearly as terrifying as thoughts of what he might do next.

Amelia came downstairs at about noon, just after he and Cole returned from loading up the last horse Jeff was going to stable for Laurel Glen. Only the family animals were left, and they'd all been moved to stable one. Cole was on the phone when Amelia came into the library, and Ross was grateful for the buffer.

"Meg said you carried me upstairs. That was unnecessary and foolish. Your shoulder isn't going to get better if you keep hauling me around like a potato sack."

He smiled at her, drinking in the warmth in her smiling eyes for the lonely days ahead, but he fought to keep any feelings other than mere friendliness hidden. "Then you're the prettiest potato sack I've ever seen," he answered, willing his voice to remain even. "And I'd like to keep it that way. I don't want you to take this wrong, but I'd like you to leave."

Chapter Sixteen

At first Amelia thought Ross was teasing, but then she saw the serious expression on his face and knew this was no joke. She stared at him, stunned into utter silence, her mind blank for several blessedly numb moments. Then the full consequence of what he'd said hit her completely. She'd lost him.

For today.

For tomorrow.

For always.

When she woke in the morning, she would wake in a different world. A world without Ross. It would be a hollow place that didn't feel like home, just another stopping-off point on a search she'd thought over. She'd finally learned that a place was not what she'd been searching for in her world travels, even though Laurel Glen had felt like home from the first.

Home was not a place but the people in that place. And anywhere she was with Ross would be home.

"Oh. Certainly," she said, at last finding her voice. She fought to maintain a neutral expression and to hide her pain. She'd already sacrificed her pride by telling him how she felt about him. She would not beg. "I'll go pack."

"It's not that you aren't welcome here," he hastened to explain. "I hope you understand that. But now that we know this guy will resort to murder, it isn't safe here at Laurel Glen. I asked Meg to go somewhere till this is over. She left earlier. She said to tell you she'd be in touch. After we catch this guy, you're certainly welcome to come back and visit her anytime you'd like."

"Visit Meg," Amelia repeated. "Yes. Of course. I—I'll go pack." Oh, dear. Hadn't she said that before? She sounded like a broken record.

Ross stood and reached toward her. "You're all right, aren't you?"

"All right?" Amelia asked, wondering what he meant. How did he think she was? She backed away, afraid if he touched her she'd shatter. She wished her voice hadn't sounded so odd. So hollow. Like her heart suddenly was.

She felt as if she'd been turned into an automaton. Like the tin man from over the rainbow, she no longer had a heart. If she resumed her world travel, while she went along, she'd have to search for a heart to replace the one she'd lost at Laurel Glen.

"Are you all right about last night?" Ross clarified. "You know you didn't kill that guy. Right? And you didn't in any way cause his death by shooting out the light. And you're okay about what you had to do to help us?"

He looked worried. And of course, he was. That was Ross. Kindhearted. Willing to take on the problems of the world. Just not willing to risk his heart by loving again. He would not lie by claiming she meant nothing to him. No. He would simply act as if they had never found each other at all.

Amelia felt her temper begin to soar. He was giving up on them. Giving up on a bright, beautiful future for them without even trying. Didn't he realize how precious what they'd found with each other was?

"Oh, sure. I'm just fine today. I explode lights and rain glass down on people I care about in life-or-death situations at least once a week. What isn't there to be okay about?" She looked at her watch and took a page out of the Taggert wisecrack repertoire. "Gee! Look at the time," she quipped. "I'd better get packed and on the road if I'm going to make it home before midnight."

When Cole slammed down the phone, Ross turned from watching Amelia's back as she practically flew out the door of his study. His son was clearly furious. "Won't Lithum Creek take Mischief?" Ross asked.

"I never got the owner on the line. I hung up. Instead I listened to that load of bunk you just shoveled at Amelia."

Ross stiffened. He hadn't thought he could hold himself any straighter. "It's not safe for her here. You know that."

"You can *visit?* What is it with you?" Cole demanded. "Do you like ripping women's hearts out?"

Ross heard the boiling anger under the surface and knew Cole was referring to what he believed about his parents' marriage. Ross forced himself to ignore it even though he was barely holding it together after watching the woman he loved all but run out of his life. Only a promise to his dead wife kept him from blurting out the whole ugly truth.

"I'm trying to keep her safe," Ross retorted. "And who are you to talk to me about breaking hearts? When you first came home we had calls practically around the clock from despondent women looking for you."

"I'm not denying I've got a problem with commitment. We're not talking about me. We're talking about you and Amelia."

"I'm too old for her. Okay? There, I said it. I should have seen it before, but now that I have, I had to make a clean break."

Cole narrowed his eyes. "Right, Dad, and you did it with all the skill of a surgeon. Only you used a hatchet! And what *is* this garbage about you being too old for her?''

Ross recited all the statistics he'd come up with earlier, and Cole laughed in his face.

''You have more energy than I do! Granny lived to ninety-five. Your father died at thirty-three of an aneurysm. You could go like that.'' He snapped his fingers in Ross's face. ''Or you could break Granny's record and live years longer than Amelia. Like Granny, you could bury me or one of these other kids you're so afraid to fail.''

Ross stared at Cole across the desk for a long moment, stymied by his son's attitude. ''I thought you didn't want Amelia and me to get together.''

''I didn't want to see a nice lady like Amelia Howard hurt if you pulled this again.''

''But I just wanted—''

''Look! Do you want her in your life or not?'' Cole demanded.

Tired and hurting to his soul, Ross pursed his lips and nodded.

''Then don't let her leave without telling her so.''

Without another word said, Ross found himself alone in his study. He sank into his chair and raked his hand across his face. Had he made a mistake? Oh, not about asking Amelia to leave for her own safety, but for cutting off his relationship with her?

Maybe he *wasn't* thinking straight. He put his head back and sighed. Man, but he was tired. He hadn't been sleeping well lately and he'd only gottcn a couple of hours sleep last night because of the intruder. He'd thrown away the chance with Amelia that he'd begged for just a few short weeks ago. Had he done it just because he was exhausted?

Ross heard voices in the foyer and jumped up to see if it might be Amelia. It was. She and Cole stood at the bottom of the staircase, her luggage at her feet. She'd packed in record time.

Cole opened his arms, and Amelia hugged him. Then she stepped back and gave him a tremulous smile. "I guess this is goodbye," she said.

"I still think this is a mistake. I know, I know—you won't beg. I can't say as I blame you," Cole said, picking up her luggage and bulky camera bag. "If I don't see you before you take off, don't be a stranger. You hear?"

"Promise. I should be along in just a minute. There's something I need to do first."

"Ycah. And you give it to him good," Cole urged as he walked through the house toward the garage where her car was parked.

Amelia stared after Cole for a long moment then shook her head and picked up the briefcase she'd set down so she could hug him goodbye.

"Amelia, I wanted to explain," Ross said, moving up behind her.

She whirled to face him and dropped her briefcase. About to swallow any pride he had and beg her to come back when it was safe, Ross stooped to pick up her leather case. A folder had fallen out and spilled papers on the floor. He blinked, hardly able to comprehend what was right before his eyes. Spread across the floor were copies of all the articles on the trouble they'd been having and the name, address and phone number of the editor of their local paper. Personal things were written there, too, like Marley and her affair that no one but Amelia knew about. There were notes on last night's brainstorming session he'd thought she slept through. These were notations that could only be for an article. An article that would kill what was left of Laurel Glen.

He shoved them back in the folder and it into the briefcase and stood. "I thought better of you. But I've been a fool before. Why change now? I don't know what you're going to gain with this article but I know what more publicity will do to Laurel Glen. I rescind my offer, Ms. Howard. You're no longer welcome at Laurel Glen. Get out."

Article? Amelia looked at the briefcase Ross shoved into her arms then into his blazing blue eyes. Was he insane? He thought all her hours of work trying to unravel the mystery of who was behind the attacks and vandalism was for a newspaper article?

Maybe she'd gotten off easy. How many years would she have continued to pay for Marley's infidelity and the damage it had done to Ross's ability to trust in those he loved? A lifetime?

"I told you I'm not a reporter," Amelia said through gritted teeth. She pulled the folder containing the raft of creased and wrinkled papers and notes from her briefcase and threw them at his feet. "The legacy of Marley Taggert lives on. For your information, I was trying to help you."

"Help me? How? By offering to drive the last nail in Laurel Glen's coffin? Help like that I don't need. I've been getting it for months already! From an enemy."

"I'm not your enemy. I just didn't want to chance saying anything in front of Cole. Look at the notes. It may save your life! Goodbye, Ross."

Amelia turned and ran. Pride and composure shattered, she veered toward the back terrace at the archway off the breakfast room, hoping to avoid seeing anyone. One kind word and she'd lose control of her dammed-up tears. But even that small consideration was apparently too much to ask. She ran smack into Cole as she rounded the corner of the house.

"Hey, I thought *you* were going to give it to *him?* From the look of you, it was just the opposite."

She looked at Cole through a sheen of tears. He was so like Ross yet so different. "Best laid plans," she said. "Your father is a pigheaded, arbitrary numskull, and I wish I'd never met him! I wish I didn't love him so much, too. Please. I have to get out of here."

And to her utter shame a sob broke free of her throat. Amelia sidestepped Cole and ran again. As she slid behind the wheel she blessed him for pulling her little Jeep out of the garage. The keys were in the ignition, and she silently thanked him again. Her hands were shaking so badly she'd never have gotten key and lock together.

Her tears threatened to break free as she stopped near the lovely old octagonal barn. She moved on to the stables and halted again. The charred timbers of number four still haunted her with visions of flame and equine terror. She shivered when her gaze rested on number two. The shadows of last night touched her heart deeply. Life was sacred, and someone nearby didn't respect it at all.

But what breached any defenses she had left was the sight of the empty practice ring where she'd come upon Ross and little Emily standing at the fence. It was there she'd first seen through the wall of toughness to that tender heart he worked so hard to keep hidden. It was there he'd patiently coaxed Amelia past her fear and taught her to ride.

Weeping openly, she drove, trying to keep her vision clear. Only a few minutes after she stopped for one last look at the beautiful Laurel Glen entrance arch, however, Amelia nearly ran off the road into a ditch. She slowed down and rolled slowly to a stop while reaching for the box of tissues on the back seat. Then, with Laurel Glen's arch in her rearview mirror, Amelia gave into the racking sobs she could no longer keep at bay.

Oh, Lord. I know You wept so You must have hurt like this. Why do people do this to each other? And why do we let them? Don't let happen to me what's happened to Ross. Let me find the trust to give my love again someday. And please, please keep him safe. Keep them all safe.

She slouched in her seat and closed her eyes against the glare of the sun, wondering if she could have done anything differently. In the final analysis, though, she knew this was not her problem but Ross's. And she was not the solution to the problem. God was.

Is that why You put me here, Father? To help You bring him back to You so You could help him? Was I wrong to fall in love with him? Did I misread my purpose here?

Somehow she knew that was not the case. God was too merciful to use her so cruelly. And it was never wrong to love someone. It was only wrong to sacrifice yourself on the altar of their pain.

Ross had been cruelly betrayed and now he expected betrayal from those he loved. Until the Lord dealt with him about it, he would continue to force others away and to live alone behind walls of his own making. She could not wait and hope for that day to come without being untrue to herself. She would not. Instead she would get on with her life.

Composed and resigned, Amelia put the car in gear and drove on to meet her life. The road ahead would be hard, but she'd traveled hard roads before. And it would be lonely. She'd already survived that, as well. She would again.

After she passed Lavender Hill, the terrain changed from rolling hills to steeper inclines and pinnacles. The road took twists and turns, with steep drop-offs to one side and rocky embankments rising high on the other. The ruggedness of this strip of road was so surprising after the gentleness of Laurel Glen that she'd stopped one day to take pictures, wanting to capture the hidden beauty of the tumultuous terrain.

A series of tight-curve warning signs alerted Amelia that she needed to slow down, but when she pressed on the brake, her foot slammed all the way to the floor, and her vehicle didn't slow a bit.

Oh, dear God, help me. I don't have any brakes!

Chapter Seventeen

Ross stood in the foyer for what seemed like hours, staring at the empty doorway Amelia had run through on her way out of his life. He couldn't seem to engage his brain. Deciding not to try, he scooped up the papers and stalked to his office, where he tossed them into the trash can. By that time he could feel every beat of his heart in his head. He sank into the chair behind the desk, bracing his elbows on the desktop.

Cradling his aching head in his hands, Ross tried to order his thoughts. Why would she do this? he asked himself. She wasn't a reporter. He knew she didn't need the money, and fame was already hers. He'd come to notice that she was kind of famous in photography circles. So why write an insider article for a little paper in East Podunk, Pennsylvania?

She'd said she was trying to help. How could another article—more publicity—help?

When no answer came to mind, Ross dropped his hands to the desk. Maybe no answer came to mind because there wasn't one! She'd had that folder in her hand when she came into his office earlier. Had she been there to ask his advice or his permission about an article?

No. There wasn't an article, Ross realized with a start. Amelia had been trying to figure out who his enemy was. He dropped his face into his hands again.

Oh, Father. I did it again. Will You please teach me to think before I open my big mouth!

Ross looked at the papers in the trash can. He snatched them up and quickly scanned them. She had figured out why the attacks were happening, if not the exact person responsible. Amelia thought it was someone he'd forced himself to put out of his mind the day Marley died—the man she'd planned to leave him and the children to marry. And now that he thought about it, he had to agree.

"Care to explain why Amelia ran past me in tears?" Cole demanded after stomping in.

Ross looked up from the papers spread haphazardly over his desk. "Because your father's an idiot," he answered, springing to his feet. He had to stop her!

He'd follow her to Atlanta if need be. He couldn't let her leave without begging for her forgiveness—

once again. For a reasonably intelligent man he could be a real idiot sometimes.

He tore through the house in pursuit. Unfortunately, by the time he got to the garage Amelia was long gone. Why had he wasted so much time before looking at her clues?

"I could have told you she'd left already if you'd waited," Cole said approaching him. "She lit out of here as if rabid hounds were after her. She said she wished she'd never met you. She also called you pigheaded, arbitrary and a numskull."

Ross winced. "Leave it to Amelia to hit the nail on the head."

"What's going on?" Cole asked. "Last I heard you were going to tell her you'd lied and that you love her."

"She dropped her briefcase, and a folder fell out." Ross raked a hand through his hair and paced toward the garage then back. He patted his pockets to see if he had his car keys. He didn't. "I thought she was writing an article about us and I freaked on her."

"Amelia? Man, you are one lousy judge of character," Cole said.

"Now there's an understatement if I've ever heard one!" Ross growled and turned away from his son to pace again but stopped short when Harry Donovan stepped out of the side door of the garage. As far as Ross knew, he had no need to be there.

"Donovan, what are you doing in the garage? You fixed Amelia's car days ago."

"Uh, I—"

Donovan's words seemed to freeze on his lips as his eyes, full of alarm, followed Cole when he stooped to look at something on the ground.

Why was Donovan so nervous? Ross took a quick breath as an image flashed in his brain. It was of a list of names in Amelia's handwriting. Amelia's list of suspects. And Harry Donovan's name had been on that list. Not just on it but circled heavily in red several times.

On the wrinkled sheets of papers Ross had scanned, Amelia had started with the idea that their enemy had a grudge against him and Cole, but Cole hadn't been home in thirteen years. Before that they'd had no incident in common serious enough to warrant this kind of viciousness except Marley's death. She'd moved on to the supposition that the man in Marley's life had lost a great deal with her death. Then Amelia had tried to decide who that man could have been by making a list of men who'd been around then and were still around now.

Cole stood and pointed toward the open garage door. Donovan spun on the balls of his feet, then took off across the terrace and around the back of the house.

"It's him!" he shouted at the same time Cole yelled something nearly identical.

Ross took off after his longtime foreman and supposed friend, wondering how Cole, who was close on Ross's heels, had come to the same conclusion he had. Cole soon passed him and executed a flying leap off the top terrace that would have done an NFL linebacker proud. He took Donovan down hard on the unforgiving stone.

Ross almost slowed, but the foreman rolled and Cole slid limp to the terrace. Ross started heading diagonally in his descent down the wide stone steps toward his injured son, forgetting Donovan, who was up and running toward the truck he'd parked at the foot of the steps.

"I'm fine. Get him!" Cole shouted, rolling slowly to his side and trying to sit up.

Ross didn't think. He reacted. He'd been Cole's first football coach, after all. He ran along the second terrace till he was above the last set of steps and dove toward Donovan. Ross caught the foreman at shoulder height, and they both went flying off the steps and over the hood of Donovan's old truck at the foot of the terrace. Both men landed in a tangled heap on the driveway on the other side of the truck.

Ross pushed himself to his feet, avoiding a couple of Donovan's sluggish punches. He dragged the other man to his feet, shoving him against the front fender of the truck. The foreman appeared dazed at first but suddenly came up swinging. Caught unaware, Ross nearly went sprawling but recovered in time to jump out of the way when the foreman aimed a kick at his knee.

Ross answered the volley by snapping a solid punch to Donovan's jaw, knocking him against the rear fender. Donovan came at Ross with a left hook worthy of a prizefighter. Ross managed to avoid most of its power with a last-second feint, and Donovan's fist glanced off Ross's cheekbone. He got in a couple good solid punches, but when the foreman went to swing again, Georgie Burk's shout stopped him midswing.

"Hold it, Donovan," Georgie ordered and stepped into view wielding one of the stable rifles.

Ross wasn't surprised that his longtime friend-turned-enemy shrank against the tailgate now that he was staring down the barrel of a Remington .308 rifle with a very angry man's finger on the trigger.

Ross stepped back, staring at Donovan. "Why?" Ross demanded. "Why after all these years together would you do this?"

"You killed Marley, and all our dreams died with her. She was supposed to be leaving you and we were gonna get married. We had plans!"

"So it was you," Ross said, wondering why he hadn't suspected back then. Maybe because Donovan had been so open in his adoration of Marley. He wasn't sure of anything except that he'd been a blind idiot.

"Yeah. Hotshot Taggert lost his wife to the second string. We were going to Tennessee to start up a nice little thoroughbred farm on the money she inherited. She even had a buyer all lined up for her parents' place so we'd be away from here.''

"She said she'd be living next door to Laurel Glen. Was she leaving the kids behind, or was I losing them, too?''

As if Ross hadn't spoken, Donovan went on reliving the past as if it were yesterday. "I found us a place and a little yearling filly. I had a real deal worked for her. A measly ten thousand. I knew she was worth way more. She had heart, she just needed the right trainer. That trainer was gonna be me. And you robbed me of that. You remember Windrift?''

Ross nodded and glanced at Georgie, who moved to a few yards beyond the tailgate. "Windrift took the Triple Crown a couple years after Marley died,'' Ross said cautiously, his eyes glued to his adversary.

"Marley didn't just die! You and that son of yours killed her!''

"Her death was an accident,'' Ross said.

"You killed her and you don't even know it! She was all upset that day. She must've been up crying all night the night before. Her big brown eyes was all red and sad. I couldn't get her to see she still had to leave you like we said she would. She was real agitated about breaking your heart and leaving the kids. Then she heard you and the boy arguing out in the practice ring. She wanted to make it up to you—with you—so she went out to help patch it up between you and Cole.''

Ross nodded. "I was in pretty bad shape myself

that day, Donovan. Out of the blue my wife had just told me she was leaving me. I tried to stop her from riding but she insisted on proving to Cole that the stallion was safe.''

"But he wasn't safe, was he?" Donovan reminded Ross with an ugly sneer on his face. "And then she was lying in the dust and saying her goodbyes to you. To you! It was *me* she loved. It should have been *me* holding her. It was bad enough watching you get rich as Croesus year after year, but then you got her inheritance, too.''

"Why wait all these years for revenge, then?" Ross asked as sirens screamed in the distance. He guessed Cole must have staggered to the house and called Georgie and the police.

"I waited because I was content with the boy acting up and driving you around the bend. Then he got sent away and you lost your son. Thought it was only fair. Poetic justice, they call it. I could live with watching you suffer all these years with him gone from home and you not able to patch things up with him.''

"That's why you were always bringing up his name and going on about Jeff's accomplishments.''

"Heh, heh, heh. And you thinking I was just missing him like you was. I hated him. But I figured he was suffering, too, losing all this and his family, too. Then some things was happening in my life and at the same time he had to take it into his head to come home, trying to patch things up with you. It was just too much to stand anymore.''

"So you set out to do what? Frame him? He was fifteen years old when Marley died. He worshiped her. He wasn't in any way responsible for her death.''

Donovan narrowed his eyes. "He was the one who wouldn't ride that killer! And it would have tore your heart out if he came home to destroy you. So I set out to frame him and destroy you. Two birds with one stone.''

Ross stared at Donovan. "You killed a man to get revenge for an accident? And cost Jeff his shot at the Olympics? That young man nearly spent the rest of his life in a wheelchair.''

"Hope and Jeff were never the targets. Shame they got in the way.''

Ross struggled to hold onto his temper. He wanted to throttle the man. "So the hay accident that nearly killed Hope was engineered, too.''

The foreman laughed again. "It was supposed to be the men who got hurt. I rearranged the pallet while they ate. They never noticed it was higher. I left one side of the stack all but hollow on the middle. Whoop! Tipped right over when it bumped the pulley.''

"I hope you're satisfied with your revenge when they condemn you to death, Donovan,'' Ross said.

Donovan smiled. "Oh, I'll be satisfied. And they can't do much to me that the cancer won't. That's the thing that's going on in my life. I'll be long gone before the state of Pennsylvania gets around to killing me. But I'll die happy knowing you're grieving again for a lost lady.''

"Lost—'' Ross felt his stomach turn to lead and his heart stutter. He grabbed the foreman by the shirt. "What did you do?''

Jim Lovell was there pulling Ross back, which was a good thing, since Donovan's only answer was laughter as a patrolman dragged him away in handcuffs.

"Brake fluid!'' Cole said from behind Ross.

He spun toward his son. He hadn't known Cole was nearby. He had only to see the look in his son's eyes to know he'd heard much of the sordid tale of his mother's infidelity.

"I promised her I wouldn't tell you,'' Ross explained, reaching a hand out to his son.

In answer Cole grabbed Ross's wrist and slapped keys in his hand. "Not now. There's a puddle of brake fluid in the upper drive that trailed out of the garage. For some reason it tipped me to him. I think he may have cut Amelia's brake lines. Go!''

Ross turned to Jim Lovell. "Which way did you come in on Indian Creek?''

"From Old Orchard Road. I didn't pass a soul. Go see if she got stopped all right. I can get your statement later.''

Ross didn't need further urging. He raced up the steps and practically dove into the front seat of

Cole's car. As he raced toward her, he prayed for Amelia's safety and that she would forgive him his foolishness. But the farther he got along Indian Creek Road the more worried he became. He tried calling her on her cell phone to warn her, but she didn't answer.

If she went much farther she'd be headed into a rough series of twists and turns that caused several accidents a year to cars not suffering from the handicap of cut brake lines. Ross started praying that she was as good behind the wheel as she was behind a lens.

Chapter Eighteen

Amelia's heart pounded as she approached the sharp curve. She reached for the ignition to turn off the engine but then she remembered the power steering. She'd lose it if she shut off the ignition. The road veered sharply left, and the promised curve was upon her.

Though she fought it, momentum forced her into the shoulder of the opposite lane. The bend reversed. The car lost purchase on the shoulder and careened across both lanes, fishtailing in the loose gravel of the right lane's shoulder. The road curved again, but she'd lost some speed, and she held to the road, avoiding the gravel. She made use of the lane for opposing traffic, which she quickly thanked God was still empty.

The road took a sharp dip and straightened out for several hundred yards, but it continued downhill, adding to the speed of her vehicle. She knew that during the next bend the road would also wend its way over a dam. There would be water on one side and a steep, rocky ravine on the other side of the serpentine causeway. It was a lovely sight at a leisurely pace, she thought, and glanced at her speedometer. But sixty-five was far from leisurely on a road like this! Quickly she took the opportunity of the straighter piece of road and turned off the engine.

Nothing happened.

Or rather, nothing changed. Amelia flipped the key on then off again, but her little car moved ever forward. She felt herself break into a cold sweat as she careened around the sharp, steep curve and toward the dam. She prayed for help, tacking on a sincere request for driving abilities she wasn't sure she had. As her front quarter panel connected with the low guardrail, the car bounced off the guardrail and off the shoulder, heading toward the ravine. The contact with the wooden guardrail had slowed her a bit, and Amelia wrestled the car back onto the road.

The road straightened again, but for not for long. There were more curves ahead. While she had the opportunity, Amelia stomped on the emergency brake.

Nothing. No resistance. Just a sharp jolt as the peddle slammed nearly to the floorboards. She knew then with nauseating certainty. Someone had rigged her car. Obviously, Ross's enemy had become hers, and she had clearly given him the keys to her car.

She remembered there was another set of sharp twists and turns ahead. There was no time to think of anything but her driving. One of the curves—Ross had called it dead man's curve—was a hairpin turn bordered by scrub pines and thick underbrush. If she went off the road there, no one would ever see her green car because the road sat about ten feet above the floor of the woods.

"Help me, Father God! I'm so afraid," she cried aloud. Terrified of flipping the vehicle, Amelia didn't even try to keep to her own lane in the hairpin, then at the apex of the curve her back tires broke free, finding little purchase when they skidded into the gravel shoulder. Skidding sideways, she saw herself tipping over at the edge of the blacktop at any second. But then by some miracle she was looking ahead at the second half of the curve when the back wheels caught, catapulting her forward and out of imminent danger.

Amelia realized she was headed uphill and prayed the grade would leach off some of her speed. And if she remembered correctly, there was a high inside wall on that bend. If she could get close enough she might be able to rub the fenders against rocks and dirt to slow herself down even more the way hitting the guardrail had done before.

As soon as she began to climb, the impossible happened. The engine accelerated the way her cruise control made it behave to maintain speed on inclines.

The car moved faster, and the next curve was in front of her. She entered it, and centrifugal force threw her into the opposite lane. Her tires gave off an unholy squeal as she fought to stay away from the guardrail lest she bounce and lose what control she had. She failed, and the scream of metal scraping metal drowned out the protest of her tires.

Then her heart leaped into her mouth. The car went up on two wheels, and she glanced down to her side at the water-filled ditch beneath her. Amelia gave the wheel a sharp yank, and she thankfully fell back down onto all four wheels again.

Then mercifully the road straightened to gentler curves. Unfortunately, Amelia was traveling at such a high rate of speed that her vehicle went airborne and sailed off even the gentlest dips in the road. And every time the wheels reconnected with the road she had to fight to regain control of its fishtailing.

Help. Oh, please, Lord. Help me, she prayed as she fought tears of dread while attempting to steer the vehicle back into her own lane.

Now that she was on a straighter section of road, Amelia tried once again to affect the speed. She flicked the cruise control on and off a few times but her speed refused to drop off. Next in a desperate bid for safety she threw the transmission into reverse thinking it might stall the car. Nothing happened. The transmission was not engaging.

One thought exploded in her mind. *I'm going to die, and Ross will blame himself.*

Ross squealed around the last curve before Indian Creek straightened out for a good mile and a half. Her tire marks all over the roadway had warned him she'd been traveling at a high speed, but he was still horrified to see Amelia take flight off a small hill about a quarter mile ahead. When she landed, the car fishtailed, leaving snakelike tracks of black rubber all over the road. He didn't get it. Why didn't she stop accelerating?

Then he remembered that Hope's car had acted up last year when the computer went. It was the identical model to Amelia's. And Donovan had worked on both cars. Hope's computer had been malfunctioning, dropping into cruise control and matching the speed it had been at when Hope engaged it last. It had also short-circuited her ignition and transmission. But Hope's car had just been fitted with new brakes. She'd been able to stop. Amelia had no brakes.

Donovan must have put the old computer board in Amelia's car. It was the only explanation Ross could come up with.

The hills had flattened out. Ross floored the gas pedal and soon drew even with Amelia, tooting his horn to get her attention.

She looked over. Her eyes were wide and frightened, her skin pale. He motioned for her to roll down her window.

"Help me, Ross. It won't turn off. And I can't get it out of gear," she screamed.

He nodded, thinking furiously. "I know. Is your cell phone handy?" he shouted. He saw her rooting on the seat next to her, then she nodded. Ross grabbed his phone. Amelia's was the last number he'd called, so dialing was a simple matter. He sped up and pulled in front of her. He planned while he waited for the call to go through.

He wasn't sure how the car would handle for her if he tried using his brakes to bring it to a stop. He didn't want to take a chance on it flipping. What they needed was to make the engine stall. Then he remembered Lake Comfort. The lake had been closed for a few years, so it would be deserted. The entrance road was almost a straight shot to the beach. There were chains across the entrance, but Cole's reinforced bumper would handle them with no problem.

It was a chance they had to take, because in another mile Indian Creek Road intersected with a busy four-lane highway. She'd never make it across without a deadly accident.

Lake Comfort had a wide, sandy beach, and the water gradually deepened. With him in front to slow her down, he could peel away at the last moment, allowing Amelia's car to go into the water where it was sure to stall. The sand should help slow them down, as well.

"I'm so scared," Amelia said when the call went through.

"Listen to me," he demanded. "There's a gravel road off to the left about a quarter mile ahead. We're going down it. Together. I'm going to drop my speed and let you hit me. Then, once we're together, I'm going to use my brakes to slow you down. There's a sandy beach and a small lake at the end of it. It's shallow, so don't be afraid. I'll peel away at the last minute. The water should stall your engine. You won't be in very deep water, so don't worry. You're going to be okay, sweetheart. I promise. Now put the phone on hands free, set it down and get ready."

Ross looked at her in the rearview mirror. She was petrified. He gave her a quick thumbs-up signal then braced himself before he slowly decelerated. She smacked into his rear bumper, sending him surging forward. They contacted then bounced apart again. The next hit they stayed together, and Ross took his foot off the gas, letting her push him along a few hundred feet.

"I'm going to start slowing us down now. Look left. See the road?"

"I see it," she said, her voice trembling.

Ross gripped the wheel tighter. He wanted so desperately to hold her and comfort her. But first he had to get her out of this safely. "Good girl. Now, when I tell you, steer toward it. If we come apart and you have to hit me a few times, don't worry. This baby can take it. We'll just keep smacking together until we're the same speed. It'll be about a thirty-degree left. Okay, now.''

They did indeed come apart then smack back together several times. The road was dead ahead. The chains that were stretched across the entrance snapped as he'd thought they would.

Seconds later, Amelia screamed. Ross looked back. Her windshield had shattered.

''Are you all right?'' he yelled toward his cell phone.

''The chain whipped back and broke the windshield. I'm afraid I can't see much.''

''You don't have to,'' he told her. ''It's a straight shot from here. I'll tell you when we're nearly at the waterline. Maybe you'd feel better if you prayed. I know I would. I'm too busy thinking about my driving right now.''

And he was. He'd managed to slow them down to forty while he'd talked to her, but his brakes were starting to smoke, and it wasn't easy to maintain control of two vehicles going thirty miles per hour over the posted speed. At last they reached the beginning of the sand, and he was able to diminish her speed more quickly because her wheels started spinning in the sand. And then he was nearly at the water's edge.

''I'll be there to get you out in a few seconds,''

he told her. "You'll hit the water soon. I'm peeling off. Now!"

He gunned the engine and cut the wheel hard to the right. His back wheels dug in, and the big SUV did a one-eighty before coming to a stop. He was out the door and on his way to the water before all the dust settled. Amelia's car had traveled into the water to the top of the wheel wells before stopping. Relieved beyond measure, Ross waded in after her, only one thought on his mind. Touching her to prove to himself she was alive. Feeling her in his arms safe and breathing.

Chapter Nineteen

Amelia closed her eyes as soon as her car came to a stop. She dropped her forehead onto the wheel and thanked God for sending help. She gave up trying not to cry. Then her door swung open and Ross's hand ran over her hair and down her back.

"You okay?" Ross asked, his voice rough with emotion.

She nodded and looked at him. Tears flooded her vision and rolled down her cheeks. "I was so scared."

"I know, sweetheart, and I'm so sorry," he said, trying to dry her tears.

She sniffled. "It wasn't your fault."

Ross winced and pressed a big navy print handkerchief into her hand. "Sure it wasn't," he muttered sarcastically.

Leave it to Ross to blame himself. Rather than

waste her breath she changed the subject. "How did you know I was in trouble?"

"Donovan confessed to the vandalism and, in a way, to last night's murder," he told her as he put one knee on the running board and hugged her to his chest. "But then he goaded me. He said he was sorry he wouldn't be around to watch me grieve again. I knew he'd done something to you. Cole had seen brake fluid in the drive. He put two and two together and realized Donovan had monkeyed with your brakes. The longer I drove looking for you, seeing your skid marks, the more worried I got. Then I caught up and saw you skimming off the hilltops and fishtailing when you landed. When I think what could have happened I—"

The terror of the past fifteen minutes welled up again. "I was so afraid." He must have heard the distress in her voice, because Ross tightened his hold and she started crying again. She felt as if a pressure valve had popped inside her, gradually easing her tension. When she subsided into little hiccuping sobs, he scooped her out of the front seat, and she looped her arms around his neck. She managed to send him a grateful smile. "You saved me."

He looked at her, his expression grim. "Don't be nice to me, okay?" he ordered through gritted teeth and sloshed toward shore with her in his arms. "I'm the reason you were in danger. I'm the reason he was still on the loose. If I'd listened to you instead of going off half-cocked, Donovan would have been arrested and you would have been safe at Laurel Glen.''

"I was due to leave by the end of the week anyway. I would have been driving it then.''

He sat her in the front seat of Cole's big SUV and stepped back. "If I'd had this whole thing with Donovan behind me, you wouldn't have been leaving.''

"I wouldn't?'' she asked, supremely confused.

"At least I hope you wouldn't.''

Ross looked toward the sound of sirens in the distance just as his cell phone rang. He muttered, "Not now,'' reached past her to the dash and picked it up. "Yeah?... She's fine... Sorry, detective... Yeah, I hear you coming. I didn't call because I just got her out of her car. It was worse than we thought. Her car's up to the top of its wheels in Lake Comfort. Donovan monkeyed with more than the brakes. I'd add attempted murder to the list you're charging Donovan with.''

Ross glanced at Amelia as if gauging her reaction to his last statement. She shivered, not wanting to think how close Donovan had come to succeeding.

"You'll send a tow truck?'' he continued. "See you in a few minutes.''

"That was Detective Lovell?'' Amelia asked.

Ross nodded. "He'll be here soon. They'll tow your car out and take it to go over it for evidence.''

She glanced at the little car that she had loved from the minute she'd first seen it on the lot. She looked away. "That's fine. Right now I don't know if I'll ever be able to drive it again."

"Then I'll get you a new one. I'm sorry I was such an idiot. You'd have been safer at Laurel Glen. If I'd given you the chance to tell me what you'd figured out, he'd have been in jail where he belongs. Then maybe I'd have gone to sleep before I stuck my foot in my mouth. I need to explain why I acted as if you mean nothing to me when you really mean everything."

She was tempted to take what he said at face value, but she had reached some pretty tough conclusions about him while she'd sat near Laurel Glen's entrance and cried. "Why did you?" she asked.

"This is going to sound so stupid. I was exhausted. I felt like I was a hundred and forty-eight and not just forty-eight. I convinced myself I was too old for you. That you'd wind up raising our kids alone. I wasn't thinking straight and I was wrong. I shouldn't have tried to push you away when it was the last thing I wanted to do."

"Oh," Amelia said. Did he know he'd referred to a future for them together? He'd buy her a new car? Their kids? He'd come a long way in less than an hour. Either that or his attitude when he'd asked her to leave had been all pretense. But that wasn't the real problem. She'd been able to accept his fear of loving her and committing to a lifetime after only weeks of knowing each other. The real crux of the matter was what he'd thought of her and the way he'd treated her after she'd dropped her briefcase.

"And I shouldn't have jumped to conclusions about all those notes you dropped, either," he went on as if he'd heard her thoughts. "Can you forgive me?"

"I already do," she said without hesitation. If she'd learned one thing from her parents it was forgiveness. The second was not to ignore a problem or make assumptions about the cause of it. "But that doesn't change what you did to me. You tore my heart out and threw me out of your life when I don't believe I ever gave you the slightest cause to think I'd betray you. I need to understand why you did that. More important, you do."

Ross grimaced and sat on the running board next to her feet. "I know why. Because of Marley. I'm such an idiot. I've ruined the best thing that ever happened to me because I kept expecting to get kicked in the teeth. And it turns out Marley wasn't as bad as I thought. From what Donovan said, she must have changed her mind about leaving. He said she insisted on riding Cole's new horse to stop the argument he and I were having. She thought it might help make up for what she'd done. She wanted to reconcile.

"The funny thing is, much as I adored her, I'm not sure I'd have agreed, after having seen the other side of her."

"Yes, you would. If you'd step in the line of fire

last night for Cole, you'd have taken her back for the kids, if not yourself. You've kept her secret for years and still are, even though you know it's damaging your relationship with Cole.''

He sighed and stood to face her. ''Well, that cat's out of the bag now. Cole was there when Donovan confessed and spewed out his whole story. But I'll deal with that later. Right now I need to find out if you'll trust me not to be such an idiot again.''

Amelia didn't know what to say. He hadn't said he loved her. He'd only hinted at marriage. And did knowing why he'd done what he did guarantee he wouldn't do it again? ''I don't know,'' she answered truthfully. ''I just don't know. How long will it be before you come upon Cole and me talking and feel jealous? How long before—'' Her voice broke.

Ross put his index finger against her lips before she could get out the rest of her thought. All thought flew out of her head when he said, ''Because I love you. And I trust you. I knew there was no article before I even looked at your notes. It was me I didn't trust. Not you.''

''But you loved Marley, and she betrayed you. How do your feelings for me change a thing?''

''Did I love her? I'm not so sure anymore. I said adored. It was more like she was the goddess I served. I worked sixteen hours a day to provide for her. I was infatuated with her. But that isn't the same. What I feel for you is so much more. I was so wrapped up in Laurel Glen. Saving it. Making it more than it had been. I never realized what was missing in our lives. Apparently Marley did.

"We didn't go places alone unless it was a social engagement she'd cooked up. Oh, I'd go and have a good time. I had a goddess on my arm. We'd laugh and talk on the way, but I never thought to take her to a movie or dinner, just the two of us. I'd call and order flowers for our anniversary and buy her gifts. I'd make sure she had lots of birthday and Christmas gifts, but because the dates were on my office calendar and I was supposed to. And those days were family occasions, even the anniversaries."

He huffed out a breath. "She never complained. If your analysis is right, she didn't know how. I can understand her turning to someone who saw *her* and not a wife and mother. I know it was wrong, but I can at least understand it now. I also realize that my world didn't collapse because of what she did or because of her death but because of the effect it had on Cole and Hope. I can't remember lying in bed missing her. Just feeling guilty that she wasn't alive. None of this is much to my credit, is it?" he asked with a grimace as if realizing he wasn't exactly pleading his case as much as making a confession. But in a way he was doing a lot to allay her fears. It was clear that he'd thought about his life a lot lately.

He caressed her cheek with the backs of his fingers. "I never took *her* on a picnic or to a concert in the park or to the museums in Philly. But you weren't gone a minute that I didn't notice the hole in my life. These last weeks there was a dark cloud hanging over Laurel Glen, but it had a silver lining. You.''

Ross bent his head, and their lips met. It was as always. Flash. Fire. Ardor at its most basic level. He backed away in seconds as breathless as she suddenly was and looking almost shocked. It had been a while since he'd kissed her. It was clear they'd both forgotten the force of their emotions.

''So, ah, are you going to put this old guy out of his misery, pretty lady?''

Amelia looked at his face and slid to the ground to stand close to him. ''I don't see an old guy. I see the man I love.''

His grin, when it bloomed on his face, was a bit sheepish. ''You're right. I don't feel old at all right now. In fact I feel about sixteen again—all nerves and hormones.'' He swallowed. ''I said something about kids. How does that sound to you?''

She shot him a wry grin. ''A bit premature, actually. Kids are something I've always wanted, but only after marriage.''

He frowned then chuckled, obviously catching her meaning. ''I told you I'm nervous. Amelia Howard, would you do me the honor of becoming my wife?''

She went up on her toes and kissed him as her answer. He wrapped his arms around her and answered her kiss with one of his own. When they broke apart they were both breathless.

"Soon," he qualified with another deep swallow. "Really, really soon."

Amelia thought he'd have kissed her again, but the state police roared down the little dirt road toward them so he tucked her under his arm and held her tight as they turned to put away the past and face the future. Together.

Epilogue

Meg Taggert smiled and sniffled a little, which might seem odd but it was entirely appropriate under the circumstances. This was a wedding, after all.

"We've come here today to bless the union of Amelia Howard and Ross Taggert," Pastor Dillon began as the happy couple joined hands in front of him.

For the ceremony they'd chosen the sunroom at the back of Laurel House where they had first been introduced for the ceremony. It was to be a quiet affair with only Hope and Cole, the pastor, of course, Hope's husband and herself, the groom's ecstatic sister.

The pastor and couple stood before the replica of Laurel Glen's arch that Jeff Carrington had commissioned for his wedding to Hope in the summer. It looked perfect against the backdrop of lattice and climbing Swedish ivy. Meg sniffled again as Amelia and Ross spontaneously looked toward each other and smiled the way only those in love do.

Today was a sunny, crisp fall day. Amelia looked more beautiful than usual, which was saying a lot. She wore happiness well. She'd chosen a simple white floor-length sheath, with a boat neck and cap sleeves. Her mother's seed pearl choker and combs were her only adornments. Her hair was swept up, her riotous curls only slightly tamed at the back of her head.

Ross wore a simple navy suit and a grin a mile wide. Meg didn't know when she'd seen her brother happier. Not perhaps since he was sixteen, just before she left home to seek fame and fortune in New York. It did Meg's heart good to know that the Lord had used her to bring these two wonderful people together. They complemented each other perfectly.

Meg watched as Cole handed his father the ring he'd carried for Amelia. She had held her breath when Ross asked Cole to be his best man, but after a glare from Amelia, Cole had graciously accepted.

Hope also handed over a ring. Ross's daughter had accepted with more enthusiasm, but Amelia had been worried that Meg felt slighted. She hadn't, of course. She and Amelia had decided having the children standing up for their father was symbolic.

There was a small reception planned for later in the day, but the ceremony was private—a family affair. Meg felt a twinge, for there was a family member missing. Of course no one knew it but her. It was her cross to bear, but her joy, as well. She had a child—a son—out there somewhere who had been raised by good Christian parents. And she loved him, though she hadn't seen him since the day he was born.

Meg sighed and smiled, taking in the tableau before her as Ross claimed his first kiss as Amelia's husband. It was lovely to see her brother happy after so many years alone.

So now her advice had brought Hope and Jeff together, and her invitation to Amelia had resulted in this lovely day, as well. And both by complete accident! Meg's gaze fell on Cole again.

Just think what she could do if she set her mind to it!

* *. * * *

*If you enjoyed SILVER LINING,
you will LOVE the next story in Kate's exciting
LAUREL GLEN series:*

MOUNTAIN LAUREL
by Kate Welsh
On sale October 2002
Don't miss it!

Dear Reader,

Didn't Ross just tire you out with his trying to handle everything on his own? No wonder he's driven his children to distraction. That's why I sent Amelia to Laurel Glen. That man just needed straightening out!

Hospitals are full of heart attack victims who have let stress destroy them, and it isn't necessary. The Lord wants us to lean on Him and give Him our worries. It's funny how hard the easy stuff is, isn't it? You'd think we'd be so ready to take the weight off our shoulders and give it to Him, but some of us hold on to the weight as if it were the most precious thing we have. It's comfortable and we're used to it. Some of us hand over our worry, then snatch it back. Still, there are those of us who try, but when we go to sleep, bam! Right next to us on the bed sit those worries. If they show up tonight, just hand them right on back. Seize the peace of the Lord and let Him do the worrying for you.

Come back to Laurel Glen in a few months and watch what happens when Cole meets his match, the kind of woman he's always run away from. The sparks really fly! Till next time.

God bless you.

Kate Welsh